# Dancing Home

## ALSO BY ALMA FLOR ADA

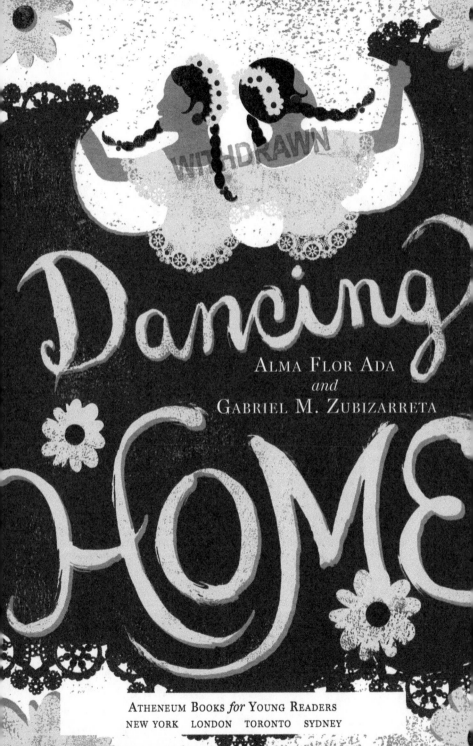

# Dancing

Alma Flor Ada
*and*
Gabriel M. Zubizarreta

# Home

Atheneum Books *for* Young Readers
New York   London   Toronto   Sydney

ATHENEUM BOOKS FOR YOUNG READERS • An imprint of Simon & Schuster Children's Publishing Division • 1230 Avenue of the Americas, New York, New York 10020 • This book is a work of fiction. Any references to historical events, real people, or real locales are used fictitiously. Other names, characters, places, and incidents are products of the authors' imagination, and any resemblance to actual events or locales or persons, living or dead, is entirely coincidental. • Copyright © 2011 by Alma Flor Ada and Gabriel M. Zubizarreta • Translation of "A Margarita" by Rubén Darío copyright © 2011 by Rosalma Zubizarreta • All rights reserved, including the right of reproduction in whole or in part in any form. • ATHENEUM BOOKS FOR YOUNG READERS is a registered trademark of Simon & Schuster, Inc. • For information about special discounts for bulk purchases, please contact Simon & Schuster Special Sales at 1-866-506-1949 or business@simonandschuster.com. • The Simon & Schuster Speakers Bureau can bring authors to your live event. For more information or to book an event, contact the Simon & Schuster Speakers Bureau at 1-866-248-3049 or visit our website at www.simonspeakers.com. • The text for this book is set in Miller. • Manufactured in the United States of America • 1113 FFG • • 10 9 8 7 6 5 4 3 • Library of Congress Cataloging-in-Publication Data • Ada, Alma Flor. • Dancing home / Alma Flor Ada and Gabriel M. Zubizarreta. — 1st ed. • p. cm. • Based on the poem "A Margarita" by Rubén Darío. • Summary: When Margie's cousin Lupe comes from Mexico to live in California with Margie's family, Lupe must adapt to America, while Margie, who thought it would be fun to have her cousin there, finds that she is embarrassed by her in school and jealous of her at home. • ISBN 978-1-4169-0088-7 (hardcover) • ISBN 978-1-4424-2396-1 (eBook) • 1. Mexican Americans—Juvenile fiction. [1. Mexican Americans—Fiction. 2. Family life—California—Fiction. 3. Cousins—Fiction. 4. Fathers and daughters—Fiction.] I. Zubizarreta, Gabriel M. II. Title. • PZ7.A1857Dal 2011 • [Fic]—dc22 • 2010013229

*To Virgilú, grateful for the inspiration,*
*and for having brought into my life a bouquet of joy:*
*Virginia Marie, Lauren, Allison, and Julia*
*—A. F. A.*

*For Camille, Jessica, and Collette:*
*May you live with the courage to learn, love,*
*and lead so as to write your own destinies.*
*Love always, Dad*
*—G. M. Z.*

# Acknowledgments

Thank you . . .

To Jessica and Camille Zubizarreta,
for being part of this story in more ways than one.

To Rosalma Zubizarreta, for her insightful contributions and
her original English version of Rubén Darío's classic poem.

To Hannah Brooks, for repeated readings
of the evolving manuscript.

To Isabel Campoy, for her unfaltering support.

To Lindsay Schlegel, for her enthusiasm in editing the
manuscript. To the excellent and supportive personnel at
Atheneum. And very especially to Namrata Tripathi,
for her invaluable presence in the creation of this book.

# Contents

# 1. The Map

Margie felt nervous having to wait outside the principal's office. She kept her eyes fixed on the huge map that covered the entire wall. Mrs. Donaldson seemed to be a pleasant woman, but Margie had never had to address the principal all by herself before.

The map's colors were vivid and bold, showing Canada, the United States, and part of Mexico. Alaska and the rest of the United States were a strong green; Canada was a bright yellow. The remainder of the map, however, showed only a small part of Mexico in a drab sandlike color Margie could not name.

For Margie, maps were an invitation to wonder, a promise that someday she would visit faraway places all over the world.

Looking at this one, Margie could imagine herself admiring the giant glaciers in Alaska, standing in awe in front of the Grand Canyon, gazing at the endless plains of the Midwest, trying to find her way in the midst of bustling New York City, or peering at the rocky coasts of Maine . . . but when her eyes began to wander south of the border, she averted her gaze. *That is not a place I want to visit,* she thought, remembering so many conversations between her parents and their neighbors, tales of families not having enough money to live a decent life, of sick people lacking medical care, and of people losing their land and homes. As she pushed those troubling thoughts aside, Margie's heart once again swelled with pride, knowing she had been born north of that border, in the United States, an American.

Margie looked over at the girl waiting in the other chair outside the principal's office. Her cousin Lupe was not as lucky as Margie, who had been born in the United States. Lupe had just arrived from Mexico and looked completely out of place in that silly frilly dress she had insisted on wearing. "My mother made it especially for me," she had pleaded, and Margie's mother had allowed her to wear it. That dress was much too fancy for school. It was so embarrassing for Margie to be seen with a cousin who was dressed like a doll!

Margie knew her classmates would tease Lupe about her organza dress and her long braids. Would all that teasing spill over to Margie? Were they going to start mocking her, squealing "Maargereeeeeta, Maargereeeeeta" and asking her when had she crossed over from Mexico? She had hated it so much when they used to tease her like that!

It had been such a struggle for Margie to get her classmates to stop thinking of her as Mexican. She was very proud of having been born in Texas. She was as American as anyone else. Now Margie feared that because Lupe was tagging along in that dumb dress, everyone would start back up with the teasing she had hated so much. She could just hear her classmates asking her why she didn't bring burritos for lunch, or looking at her and laughing as they said, "No way, José!"

Margie was still wishing she could have convinced Lupe to dress normally when the principal appeared, walking briskly and motioning for the girls to follow her into her office.

"Good morning, Margarita. What can I do for you?" Mrs. Donaldson's voice was all business. Everything about her seemed to say, *I do not have a minute to spare.*

"Good morning, Mrs. Donaldson. This is my cousin Lupe. She just got here from Mexico. My mother said—"

Mrs. Donaldson, who had begun to shuffle the papers on her desktop, interrupted Margie: "Your mother registered her yesterday, Margarita. Just take her with you to your class."

"To *my* class?" There was surprise and urgency in Margie's voice. "But she just got here. She is from Mexico. She doesn't know how to speak."

Mrs. Donaldson stared at Margie. "You mean she doesn't know how to speak English, right? I imagine she can speak Spanish." Then, turning to Lupe, she slowly said, *"Bien—ve—ni—da* to Fair Oaks, Lupe. *Bonito vestido."*

Lupe managed a shy smile, but she kept looking down at her feet and answered in the smallest voice, *"Muchas gracias—"*

Margie cut through Lupe's words. "Well, yes, she speaks Spanish. But in my class we only speak English. She is not going to fit in there, Mrs. Donaldson." She was shocked at her audacity in arguing with the principal, but there was no way she was going to show up in class with her Mexican cousin tagging along. Why had Mrs. Donaldson complimented

Lupe's stupid party dress? How could adults be so dishonest? Margie wondered.

Mrs. Donaldson said firmly, "The fifth-grade bilingual class is overbooked. There is no way I can put one more desk in there. Judging by her grades in Mexico, Lupe is a very good student, and since you can help her, both here and at home, we all expect that she will do well in your class." And with a voice that left no room for a reply, she added, "I thought you would be happy about this. She is your cousin, Margarita!"

Mrs. Donaldson looked so stern that Margie decided not to say anything else. She got up and left, signaling Lupe to follow her. But as she was leaving the office, she looked back at the huge map of the United States. This was a great country, and she was very glad that she had been born here and spoke English as well as any of her friends.

Lupe followed Margie down the hall. She had not understood the conversation in the principal's office. It was clear to Lupe that her cousin was upset, but Lupe did not know why. As they made their way to the classroom, everything Lupe saw awakened her curiosity. It was all so different from Mexico! She had never been to a school with so many things hanging on the walls. And she still could not believe that the students didn't wear uniforms. She had been very surprised when her aunt told her. When Lupe arrived in California, Tía Consuelo had bought her some new clothes to wear to school. But for this first day Lupe had wanted to wear the pink organza dress her mother had made. Margie did not seem to like it, but Lupe felt it was important to give a good first impression.

When Margie opened the door, Lupe's surprise grew. They were obviously in a classroom, but instead of the neat rows of desks that she was used to, the students were sitting in small clusters of two or four desks placed around the room. And there were all sorts of different things in the classroom—posters on the walls, mobiles hanging from the ceiling, many different kinds of books on the book-shelves. There was even a fish tank! With binders and backpacks scattered all over, it looked very chaotic, more like a bus station than a classroom.

Stunned, Lupe hesitated in the doorway, afraid to walk in. Glancing at everything from the corners of her eyes, she remembered the neat and orderly classroom of her old school in Mexico. Suddenly she became aware that everyone in the room was looking at her. She dropped her gaze and stared down at the floor in front of her feet.

Meanwhile, Margie went directly to the teacher's desk.

"Miss Jones, this is my cousin Lupe González. Mrs. Donaldson told me to bring her here. But there must be some mistake. She should be in a bilingual class, right?"

The teacher did not answer Margie's question but turned to address Lupe. Margie looked back at Lupe, who had not moved, trying to signal her to come in. Finally, Margie walked back to the door and took hold of her cousin's arm. Lupe jumped a little when Margie grabbed her, and the class was instantly filled with laughter. Lupe raised her eyes and saw that her cousin's face had turned crimson.

Obviously upset, Margie led Lupe over to Miss Jones's desk.

*"Buenos días, Lupe. ¿Cómo estás usted?"* Miss Jones said slowly, pronouncing each syllable of the formal greeting.

Surprised at being addressed so formally, Lupe did not know how to answer the teacher's halting Spanish. But she knew how to show respect, so she looked down. More laughter spread around the room.

"Margie, have your cousin sit next to you, in the back of the class, so that you can translate what I say. That is all the Spanish I know."

"But Miss Jones . . ." The urgency in Margie's voice was greater than ever. "I don't know much Spanish myself. I won't be able to translate everything you say. Besides, I sit up front, next to Liz."

"I have moved you next to the empty seat in the back. That way you can translate while I speak and you won't disturb the rest of the class. Now go sit down, class should have started already. And please tell your cousin that even if she is feeling shy, she needs to look at me when I am talking to her."

Margie sulked toward her new seat, while Lupe continued to stand in front of the teacher's desk. When the laughter started up again, Margie turned and grabbed Lupe, pulling her toward the back of the class. Lupe followed silently. When she dared to look up and smile, the laughter started again, until Miss Jones demanded silence.

While Miss Jones talked on and on about the Pilgrims, Margie searched for the words in Spanish to translate what the teacher was saying. But there was no way she could even begin to convey the half of it, and so she remained silent instead. Lupe looked expectantly at the teacher for a moment, but then she busied herself turning the pages of the history book and looking at the illustrations.

Margie felt deeply hurt. She had always liked sitting up front. And Liz was her best friend. Now she had to sit at the other end of the room, while Betty sat next to Liz. Margie could see them chatting and smiling as if they were already best friends.

Margie had joined in the family excitement when her mother announced that her cousin Lupe was coming to stay with them. Margie had no brothers or sisters, and since none of her school friends lived close by, she thought it might be fun to have someone to hang out with at home. Besides, Lupe could help with the chores—washing and drying dishes and cleaning and straightening the kitchen after dinner would be less boring if the two of them were working together. But above all Margie had hoped that once Lupe was here, it would be easier to convince her mother to let her visit Liz and go out to the mall.

Margie had not thought at all about how having Lupe here might affect her life at school. She had imagined parting ways at the school door, Lupe going to the bilingual classroom and Margie going to her own classroom with her friends.

"Margie! Are you listening to me?" Miss Jones sounded angry. Everyone was staring at Margie, who again felt her face getting warm. "When are you going to start explaining to your cousin what I have been saying?"

"But I told you, Miss Jones. I don't know that much Spanish. I was born in Texas." Margie's voice could hardly be heard, but what could be heard loud and clear was the laughter coming from John and Peter, the two boys sitting on her right.

"Enough!" Miss Jones gave John and Peter one of her silencing looks. "Take out your math workbooks."

Margie felt confused. How could things change so quickly? She had felt so comfortable in this class, and now everything seemed out of control. She looked down at her math workbook, although the numbers looked so blurry that she could hardly read them.

During the exchange between the teacher and her cousin, Lupe never raised her head. Even though she did not understand the words, she knew they had to do with her, and she felt so embarrassed that she buried her face in the history book. What she really wanted was to crawl under the desk, or better yet, to run all the way back to Mexico.

Miss Jones walked to the back of the room and placed an open workbook on Lupe's desk. Lupe looked down at the numbers on the page and smiled. Finally, here was something she knew how to do! She took out her pencil and began to add, subtract, multiply, and divide, while Margie worked, much more slowly, on a similar page.

When she finished the last equation, Lupe turned the page. But on the next page there were no numbers, only words. She looked at Margie, but Margie was not even halfway down the first page.

Lupe felt lost again and her eyes became moist with tears.

When Miss Jones came to her desk to look at her work, Lupe turned to the page she had completed.

"Excellent!" the teacher exclaimed, pleased. "¡Excelente!" She held the page up for everyone to see. Then she added, "Margie, would you please translate the word problems on the next page for her?"

But Margie looked up from the workbook and shook her head. "I can't, Miss Jones. Really, I can't."

Miss Jones found Lupe another page with numbers and returned to the front of the class.

While the teacher walked back to her desk, Lupe was looking at Margie's work. She pointed to one of the solutions Margie had written and said to her, *"No es así."* Lupe heard a small laugh from the boys and a *"No excelente,* Maaargaaaareeetaaa." Again she looked down and blushed, wishing she had not said anything at all.

At lunchtime Margie and Lupe were at the end of the line. Lupe saw Margie look for a seat near the girl with the curly hair, but when they finally got their food, all the other seats were filled. Lupe and Margie were forced to sit at the opposite end of the table.

A few times during lunch Lupe tried to say something, but Margie silenced her. Lupe ate quietly. Margie left most of her food on the tray.

# 2. Going North

When Lupe had answered the knock on the door, she had been very surprised to find a woman she had never seen before. Lupe knew most of the people who lived in her small town. But while she was sure she did not know this woman, she looked very familiar.

It was easy to see her clothes were smarter than what the other women in town wore. And though the woman had long hair, just like they all did, she did not wear it braided, but had it collected in a twist at the back of her neck.

The woman looked at Lupe for a moment in silence, and then she smiled and exclaimed, "Lupe! You are Lupe, right?" and, without waiting for an answer, she wrapped Lupe into a tight embrace.

"I'm Consuelo, your aunt from California."

Lupe could hardly believe her ears. She had never met her aunt, though she'd always longed to do so.

Lupe smiled, not sure what she should say. But her aunt had plenty to say for both of them.

First she asked about Lupe's mother. When Lupe answered that her mother had gone to the market with her twin little brothers and her aunt Rosalía, Tía Consuelo directed Lupe to a chair and sat herself down in another.

"Lupe, I am here to ask you if you would like to come with me to California. I'm your father's only sister, you know."

Her father . . . no one had spoken to Lupe of her father in a long time. A few years back, like many of the other men from town, her father, Juan, had gone to *el Norte*. He sold the family's plot of land to pay for the trip and promised to send money so that everything would be better for everyone. He went to Stockton, California, to work in the asparagus fields. Lupe's mother, Dolores, had not wanted him to go, but he was determined.

Dolores was relieved when she got the first letter from Juan, letting her know he had been able to make it to California. For a few months he sent letters and some money. But after several months no more letters came and no more money arrived. Because Juan had crossed the border without the right papers, Dolores could not expect him to come back for a visit, but she had not anticipated that he would stop sending them money or at least news about himself.

Lupe missed her father, who had been so full of life and never seemed too tired to carry her on his back or to swing her up in the air until she could almost touch the ceiling. She missed the wonderful stories he liked to tell at night. Stories where he was always the hero, capable of fighting monsters and rescuing those in need. Most of all, she missed going to sleep listening to him softly playing beautiful ballads on his guitar. Those songs had filled the house and her sleep with gentle dreams. When he was gone, the house became sad and silent.

After her father left, Lupe often heard her mother crying at night. Although she did not say anything to Lupe, Lupe knew her mother feared that Lupe's father might be sick or even dead.

Everyone in the family helped in various ways, some sharing vegetables from their own small fields and others bringing groceries from the store. Lupe's mother worked, brushing and washing wool fresh from the sheep. But there never seemed to be enough of anything—money, food, or clothes.

When her father had been away for almost three years, someone came back from Stockton and mentioned that Lupe's father had left California. He knew someone who had seen him in Chicago, and there were rumors that he now had another family.

At first Lupe's mother became very depressed. She stopped looking for work and cried all the time. Then she stopped cooking and would tell Lupe to go eat at her grandmother's. After a few weeks of this she started working herself into a frenzy. She cleaned the house from end to end and gave away every last thing that had belonged to Lupe's father— an old pair of work shoes, some old shirts. Finally she began to look for work in earnest and was quickly hired by one of the largest rug weavers to help prepare wool on a full-time basis.

After that Lupe hardly ever saw her mother, as she would leave the house very early in the morning and not return until nightfall. Lupe had all her meals at her *abuelita* Mercedes' home. Lupe felt as if her mother did not want to see her, as if she was one more thing that her father had left behind and that now only brought painful memories of the past.

About two years ago, when Lupe came home from school one day, her mother introduced her to a man who had come to live in their house. Without really looking at Lupe, her mother said, "This is Felipe, your new father." The man hardly looked at her either.

There was no question that Lupe's mother was happier. She spent more time at home. And Lupe now had her meals there also, instead of at her grandmother's. Only, her house did not feel so much like home anymore.

A year later Dolores had twin boys.

The arrival of Lupe's baby brothers was the most joyful thing that had happened in a long time. Lupe was delighted by how soft and beautiful the babies were, and marveled at their tiny hands and feet. She loved taking care of Pedro and Pablo and did not mind being the one who washed their clothes and fed them.

Watching them grow, observing small changes every day, filled her with excitement. And now that she and her mother both shared a love for the boys, a new bond seemed to be forming between them.

Sometimes her mother would do something special for Lupe, brushing her hair, cooking one of her favorite dishes, or sewing her a new blouse. But those moments were few and far between. And

Lupe missed the times when her mother taught her embroidery, how they used to chat together about so many things, and especially the pride her mother used to show whenever Lupe brought home good grades from school.

Some nights, lying awake, Lupe felt like she was no longer her mother's daughter. It felt as if she was simply becoming her mother's friend.

Twice a year, at Christmas and on her birthday, a package always arrived for Lupe from the United States. It was never from her father, but instead from the aunt whom she had never met, the woman who now sat across from her. Thanks to those packages, Lupe had had new dresses and skirts, T-shirts, socks, and running shoes.

Now here was this unknown aunt, talking about taking her to California.

"Your cousin Margarita, my daughter, is your own age. You two can play and go to school together. It will be very good for you to learn English."

The words shocked Lupe and set off a deep ache in her heart. Leaving her town would mean saying good-bye to the twins. It would mean leaving behind many other people too, particularly her kind *abuelita* Mercedes and her other relatives, just like her father had done. Yet somehow the invitation also meant escaping the awkward feeling of being a stranger in her own home. She was no longer a little girl, and there was a new family in her house. She always felt uneasy in front of the twins' father, and she knew that he felt uncomfortable with her also, particularly whenever he and Lupe's mother argued.

Lupe knew she had helped her mother in many ways, but maybe now it was time to go. Deep down Lupe also secretly hoped she might somehow find her father.

When Tía Consuelo finished telling her about how her husband, Tío Francisco, would also be very happy to have her come, and about the many things she would get to see in California, Lupe asked her, surprised at her own directness, "And my father, do you know where he is?"

Lupe had the feeling that her aunt had been anticipating that question. She answered firmly, "No, Lupita. It is very sad. But I do not know where your father is. I had been in the United States for several years before Juan went to California. I don't know why he didn't look for me. Maybe he thought I would remind him of how I had encouraged him to study, advised him to wait before getting married . . . or perhaps he was afraid I'd ask him why he sold our land without talking with me about it. By the time he went north, I would have been able to help him. I was already married, and your *tío* Francisco is a very kind person. But I didn't know Juan had left until one of your mother's brothers wrote to me, asking about him. And I have never heard from him. I am so sorry."

As she listened to her aunt, tears flowed from Lupe's eyes.

Tía Consuelo added: "It's very sad that he has not been in touch and it must be especially hard for you. But Lupita, people without legal papers usually pay all of their money just to get into the United States. Often they end up in debt to the *coyotes* who bring them across the border. It's difficult to find work, and many of the jobs they find are only temporary and uncertain. They have to work for very low wages and people often take advantage of them. Many times they rent beds in crowded rooms until they can save enough money to pay their debts. And always they are afraid that they may be captured by the immigration authorities and sent back across the border. Living in fear leads people to do things they may not otherwise do. What he did to you was not right; however he was probably in a very difficult situation."

Lupe wiped away her tears with the back of her hand. She felt that the sadness in her aunt's voice somehow gave her permission to express her own secret hurt. One of the hardest things about her father's absence had been not being able to talk about it with anyone.

"And what does my mother say? Have you spoken to her?"

"No, Lupe. I wanted to ask you first," Tía Consuelo responded, and then she added, "There is one person I have spoken with, though. I went to visit your *abuelita* Mercedes. She thinks it is a good idea. She loves you very much, Lupe. And although she would be sad to see you go, she is sure this is best for you."

Lupe thought about Abuelita Mercedes, her mother's mother, who had been her refuge many times when her mother was away from home. Abuelita Mercedes had been the only constant presence in Lupe's life during that time. Her grandmother had not only fed her but also shown her kindness in many ways. There were often special treats waiting for Lupe when she returned from school in the afternoon. And Abuelita Mercedes always wanted to know what Lupe had learned in school each day. Sometimes, particularly if her mother was late in coming to pick her up, Abuelita Mercedes would tell wonderful stories that always kept Lupe enthralled, even if she had already heard them before.

Lately, though, her grandmother's health had been poor, and she had moved in with one of Lupe's uncles. There were many little grandchildren, Lupe's cousins, to care for in that house, and they kept Abuelita Mercedes busy.

"If Abuelita thinks it's all right, I think I would like to go." Lupe said the words so softly her aunt could hardly hear them. But the shy smile on Lupe's face confirmed that the offer had been accepted.

All of the arrangements for the trip had already been made. Lupe would be able to go to the United States with a proper visa.

Tía Consuelo explained that she had started working for a lady who traveled to Mexico from time to time. This lady was traveling to Oaxaca for a month and had asked Tía Consuelo to accompany her. Since the lady's brother worked for the U.S. Consulate in Mexico City, and because Lupe's uncle and aunt were now U.S. citizens, they had been able to help Lupe obtain a student visa.

Lupe's mother was surprised by the idea of having her daughter travel to the United States, but after a conversation with her own mother, Abuelita Mercedes, Dolores agreed to let Lupe leave. Then she took on the serious task of sewing Lupe a fancy organza dress, the dress Lupe insisted on wearing on her first day of school in California. Making that very special dress was Dolores's way of letting Lupe know how much she loved her. Wearing it was Lupe's silent way of honoring her mother and holding her close to her heart.

# 3. Being American

During the next few weeks Margie tried her best to satisfy her teacher's requests to translate for Lupe. Her mother also kept encouraging her to help her cousin, but no matter how much Margie would have liked to do so, she kept struggling to find the right words. The frustration of not being able to do what was being asked of her made her sulk more each day.

When a space opened up in the bilingual classroom and Miss Jones asked her to take Lupe to Mrs. Rodríguez's class, Margie felt very relieved.

That afternoon, sitting in the kitchen while her mother brushed and braided Lupe's long hair, Margie tried explaining, "It will really be better for her, Mom, she will be able to understand everything while she learns English."

"*Sí, m'hijita*, it will be okay, *todo saldrá bien*," replied her mother, smiling softly as she kept brushing Lupe's hair. When the braids were finished, tied with brilliant red ribbons and hanging thick and long on Lupe's back, Tía Consuelo asked her niece to pick some lemons from the lemon tree in the backyard and take them to their neighbor Señora Juárez.

After Lupe left, Margie's mother said, "Why do you keep telling the teacher you don't speak Spanish, *m'hijita*? Spanish was the first language you spoke. Spanish is the language of your *abuelitos* and your *tíos y tías*. Spanish is the language of your father. My language. Don't you see? Speaking two languages is better than having just one."

"But we live in America, Mom. This is an English-speaking country. Live in America, speak American. That's what they all say." Margie looked at her mother's anxious face. What use was there in arguing? They had gone over it so many times. "I'm going to do my homework, okay?" Margie rushed upstairs to her room.

Lying on her bed, Margie thought once more about speaking Spanish. Maybe she had spoken Spanish well when she was three. As well as a three-year-old could speak, at least. Then she had started going to the Head Start Program, and from then on she switched to speaking English. She seemed to remember that once upon a time her parents had been very proud of that. And now, yes, she understood most of what her mother told her to do around the house in Spanish. But when her mother and father went on talking forever among themselves, or when her mother spoke with her aunts, she hardly understood anything. And certainly, trying to speak Spanish was useless. What was the point of it, anyway? The language of the country was English, right? English was the language of anyone who amounted to anything. Still, it bothered her that the whole issue upset her so much.

During the next few days Margie realized that contrary to what she had hoped, not having Lupe in her class did not bring things back to normal. Margie asked Miss Jones to move her back to her old seat, but Liz and Betty had become best friends, and Betty did not want to be moved. So Margie continued to sit at the back of the class, all by herself, next to John and Peter.

Neither of the boys missed an opportunity to taunt her. "How's your cousin, Maaaargaaaareee-taaaa?" Her mispronounced name seemed to get longer each time Peter asked the question, mocking the name that Margie had abandoned in third grade.

Why couldn't he just stop teasing her, like most of her classmates had?

John was even nastier. Throughout the day he would ask her, "Has your cousin dried her back yet? Can she talk?" Or, "Did she leave her tongue behind in Mexico?" And Peter would laugh as if it were the first time he was hearing those words instead of the millionth time.

Margie knew what it felt like to be alone and not fit in. She had felt alone before, when they had just moved here from Texas and she didn't know anyone. She had managed to fit in by changing her name and making friends with Liz. She thought she'd learned to cope with the other kids' teasing, but now she was surprised that the taunting was still able to hurt her so deeply. Perhaps what she'd done was change only enough so that she could pretend to blend in.

Now that the name-calling had started again, she found it bothered her even more than before, because now it was directed not only at her, but also at Lupe. Margie knew she had not been nice to Lupe. She had not tried to help her feel welcome. And the worst part was that she knew what Lupe must be going through.

But why did they have to pick on someone just

for being different? Didn't they realize how difficult it was to have to learn a new language and live in a new environment? Lupe was dealing with having been separated from her family; wasn't she deserving of kindness and compassion, or was that not important because she was different?

John and Peter were so proud to be American, to have the privilege of living in this rich, powerful country. But did being American mean that you bullied anyone who wasn't?

# 4. Braids

At school the empty seat next to Margie kept tugging at her conscience. It was as if Lupe had never left the class and was still there, waiting for her cousin to help her.

In contrast to her absence in the classroom, it seemed to Margie that Lupe took up quite a bit of space at home. Lupe loved to hear family stories and never tired of listening to her uncle talk about his childhood. Margie's father talked about how he used to follow the crops with his family, and told stories about his first jobs outside the fields, and the evening classes he took because he was determined to study all he could. Lupe was enthralled, while Margie could hardly follow her father's enthusiastic Spanish.

Margie's father also talked about life in Mexico, explaining how his own father, Margie's grandfather, Abuelito Rafael, had started coming to the United

States with the Bracero Program, which brought Mexican farmers to plant and tend the fields not only in California and the Southwest, but throughout the country.

This program had started when many of the old family farms in the United States were bought up by large agricultural enterprises. These new factory farms needed many seasonal workers. Since few people in the United States were willing to do this kind of low-wage work, laws were passed allowing growers to bring men from Mexico to do farmwork in the United States and then return to Mexico. These seasonal workers were called braceros.

Margie's father taught Lupe some of the *corridos de braceros*, the ballads that the braceros would sing during their long train rides across the United States. The *corridos* told of the braceros's plight, their nostalgia for everything they had left behind, and mentioned the places where they were going. It was as though these workers, so far away from home, were frightened of being swallowed up by this enormous country, so they sang their stories in hopes that their news would somehow reach their loved ones.

Whenever her father noticed that Margie was listening, he would include a sentence or two in

English: "Margarita, I'm telling her about such and such a time. You know the story." Then he would continue in the deep and rich Spanish words that Margie could not fully understand.

Margie did know some of the stories, but they had never felt as fascinating before as they did now that her father was telling them to Lupe in Spanish. Margie tried to follow along, but she would quickly get tired of trying to understand and become annoyed when her parents and Lupe would suddenly burst out laughing and she could not figure out why. She wasn't about to ask, either. She had asked them once to explain a joke, but their explanation hadn't made any sense to her. Instead, it had only made the others laugh more. When they were talking like this, it felt as though her mother and father were more Lupe's parents than her own.

Above all, Margie missed the way her father used to speak about his day at work, making references to things that the three of them (back when it had been just the three of them) had done together. Now all of his stories seemed to be rooted in the past.

And then there were the braids. For Margie, Lupe's braids had become a symbol of all the changes that were making her life so difficult.

At the beginning of the school year Margie had convinced her mother to let her get a perm. Liz had a wonderful head of brown curls, which Margie saw as the ideal image of a true American girl. Margie's mother had tried to assure her that her straight black hair was beautiful, but Margie had pleaded and pleaded until her mother had reluctantly given in to her request.

Now her mother took a long time every morning and every afternoon brushing and braiding Lupe's hair. And while she was always willing to listen to Margie tell stories about what had happened at school that day, their conversations did not seem to have the kind of intimacy that her mother could convey just by touching and stroking her cousin's long hair.

# 5. Dreams and Nightmares

Lupe's days were so full with new experiences, she had little time to think about the past. School was very different from what she had known in Mexico. At home the teacher had stood at the front of the classroom and spoken most of the time. The students listened, and sometimes they copied what the teacher wrote on the board into their notebooks. Occasionally a student would be asked to go to the board and solve a math problem or write a sentence and analyze it. But for the most part, students sat quietly in neat rows and listened, read, or wrote, with very little talking to one another except in whispers behind the teacher's back.

In Mrs. Rodríguez's class the students sat in groups of four. They were encouraged to work cooperatively, to talk about their ideas with one another, and to discover new information and solve problems together. They had many opportunities to get up and move around the classroom and to do research using books or computers.

Lupe enjoyed the interaction, but she had not quite gotten used to it yet. Sometimes she missed the security provided by the order and structure of her old school. At the same time, she realized that with each day in Mrs. Rodríguez's class she felt more comfortable with the changes. As her *abuelita* used to say, *"Lo que no te mata, te hace más fuerte,"* what doesn't kill you makes you stronger.

It was particularly frustrating for Lupe to try to do her schoolwork in English. During her time in Margie's class she had felt continually embarrassed and convinced that everyone thought she was stupid. Before, in Mexico, her teachers and her classmates had seen her as a smart girl. She had gone from being one of the best students in her class to being someone who was not able to do almost any of her classwork, except for the math problems.

In the bilingual class she was in now, Lupe thrived during the periods taught in Spanish. But when the class was conducted in English, she still felt lost most of the time. Although she learned new words and seemed to understand much more every day, it was still hard for her to communicate in English. She did not dare to try speaking because she was sure she would make mistakes. The teasing she had experienced those first few weeks had made her afraid of giving people any more reason to make fun of her.

At this new school Lupe realized for the first time how much she loved her home language. She felt so pleased whenever the teacher used one of the songs or poems that she had learned during her first years of school, or when one of her classmates knew one of the jump-rope chants and rhymes that Lupe and her friends had sung at home when they had played during recess.

For Lupe, what was hardest about being surrounded by a new language was the feeling of being left out. She disliked not knowing when something was funny and not understanding what it was that people were laughing about. In this new language it was hard to tell whether something had been said as a joke or with sarcasm. She felt like a scared kindergartner instead of like one of the best students in fifth grade, as she had been in Mexico.

Lupe began having strange dreams. One particular nightmare kept coming back again and again, at least once a week. In it Lupe was supposed to be reciting a poem in front of the whole school during one of the Friday cultural assemblies they used to have at her old school in Mexico. Lupe had loved those assemblies and had always been happy when she was asked to recite. But in the dream the people listening were not her old teachers and classmates in Mexico, but the ones here in her new school in California. When Lupe began to recite her poem, she moved her lips but no sound came out of her mouth, only silence. Finally she began to quack like a duck, and then she'd wake up in a cold sweat. She knew it was a silly dream, but it kept happening again and again.

Other nights she dreamt that as she walked through her old school, the uniform she used to wear began to fall off, first the skirt, then her blouse, until she was wearing only her cotton slip. Just then the bell rang, and all of her old classmates came out of their classrooms and stared at her in disbelief. There was no place to hide. She would always wake up from this dream with a start, and with the feeling that nothing in her life made sense anymore.

Once or twice she had even had a dream where everything was upside down and inside out: The furniture was on the ceiling, cats were barking and dogs were meowing, and the canary her *tía* Consuelo kept in the family room was speaking with the voice of the parrot that had perched in her *abuelita* Mercedes's kitchen.

Whenever Lupe woke up from one of her dreams, she'd look around her room in the dim glow of the night-light her aunt had installed for her. This room was much larger and nicer than the one she had before, but what she loved most about it was the feeling of safety she experienced here. She felt safe from her mother's crying and anger, or even worse, her absence. She was glad to know that she would never have to fear her stepfather stumbling into the house late at night after drinking with his friends, as had started to happen during the last few months she lived in Mexico, nor would she have to listen to her mother's complaints and the fights that would follow.

Yet as much as she loved feeling safe here, there were moments when she was filled with pangs of nostalgia. She missed her twin brothers, the good times when her mother was happy, her *abuelita*. She missed the mountains that surrounded the town, the fields of corn waving in the breeze, the sheep grazing up the hills, as well as the *chapulines*, the cicada-like insects children caught in the fields and brought home to be fried and turned into a very special treat.

Lupe had not had many close friends in her hometown. Sometimes she'd wondered if the pain she carried kept other children away. Nonetheless, Lupe had enjoyed doing well in school and playing with her classmates during recess. Some nights when she woke up in her new room in California, the only way she could fall back to sleep was to repeat in her mind some of the songs they used to sing on the school playground:

*A la víbora, víbora de la mar,*
Oh, here's to the serpent, the serpent of the sea,
*por aquí pueden pasar.*
if you can tag me, you will be set free.

Or the lullaby her *abuelita* used to sing to her little cousins:

*Palomita blanca, reblanca,*
Little white dove, oh little white dove,
*¿dónde está tu nido, renido?*
where is your nest, your own little nest?

*En un pino verde, reverde,*
Up in a green pine tree, oh so very green,
*todo florecido.*
a flowering green pine, the loveliest you've seen.

Then she would drift back to sleep with memories of Abuelita Mercedes and her little brothers, and the thought that she would someday gather happiness as she had once gathered wildflowers on the hillsides that surrounded her hometown, high above the cornfields below.

Other nights she would think about all the things for which she was grateful. Tía Consuelo was as loving to her as her own mother had been during her early years. Lupe had longed so much for that motherly touch, and now she was receiving a great deal of it. Tío Francisco's stories and attention also filled some of the emptiness her father had left in her life. Although Lupe still hoped to find her own father someday, it felt as though she had found a part of him that she had longed for so much. At times she worried that Margarita might resent sharing her parents with her. Lupe felt so grateful for this new home she had that she could not bear the thought of her own joy causing anyone else pain. She hoped that Margarita knew that in sharing her own parents, she was not losing anything. If need be, Lupe would find a way to help her see that.

Back home Abuelita Mercedes would always say, *"Tienes que cuidar lo que quieres mantener."* And Lupe was determined to do just that, to take good care of what she wanted to keep.

# 6. A Few Surprises

Fall had arrived and the mornings were cool. Margie was happy to have a cup of steaming *chocolate caliente* and a dish filled with *pan dulce* waiting for her at the breakfast table. One good thing that had come from having Lupe stay with her family was that her mother had gone back to making Mexican food much more frequently. And although she would have hated to admit it—since, after all, she had been the one to insist that they eat American food—Margie loved her mother's Mexican cooking.

"I gave Lupe permission to stay after school on Tuesdays and Thursdays to join the *folklórico* dance group," her mother said to Margie in her slow, deliberate English. "Please, Margarita, stay with her. You two can walk home together. Maybe use the time at school to get your homework done."

Margie bit into a piece of *pan dulce* and took a moment to think. Should she argue about yet another change in her routine? She was about to do so, but then she thought twice about it. There was no real advantage to coming home early. She had tried several times to have a long talk on the telephone with Liz, as they used to do a few months earlier, but now Liz always had homework, or had a friend over, and was impatient to get off the phone. Maybe Margie could spend some time in the library and check out the stacks at her leisure. Finding a good book was always a treat.

"Fine, Mom," Margie said, and then, wanting to see her mother smile, she added, "This *pan dulce* is really nice."

As she got up from the table to join Lupe, who was already at the door, she stopped next to her mother and lifted her face. The kiss on her cheek from her mother's soft lips stayed with her all the way to school.

That day Miss Jones had two important announcements. First of all, a new student was joining the class.

*Please, let the new student be a girl,* wished Margie.

Miss Jones also announced that they all would

be doing a final project for their last year in elementary school.

Just then Mrs. Donaldson came into the classroom and introduced a tall blond girl named Camille.

*I hope Miss Jones sits her next to me,* Margie thought, and looked at the empty desk where Lupe used to sit.

As if following Margie's glance, Miss Jones asked Camille to sit next to Margie.

*Great!* thought Margie. *Now I have someone between me and John and Peter.*

As she sat down, the new girl said, "Hi, I'm Camille." A bright smile filled her face.

"Hi. I'm Margie," said Margie as she smiled back with relief. Then she thought, *I think I have just lucked out! She seems really nice.*

Once the girls were settled, Miss Jones began talking about the project again.

"I know most of you kept journals last year, and this project involves keeping a journal too. However, this year's journal will have a specific purpose. I'm glad I am explaining this project today; now Camille can get started right along with everyone else.

"Each of you will use a journal to jot down ideas about a topic of personal interest. Not something that other people might think is important, but something that is truly important to you."

Miss Jones explained that later they would be using these notes and reflections to write a final product. Since they were completing elementary school, they might choose to write an essay about what they had learned and how they had learned it. Or they might write a poem, or even a letter—for example, a letter to their future self, to the person they might be once they finished middle school.

"It's okay to write down your first thoughts in your journal, since the journal will be a starting point. Then I want you to reflect, to keep thinking, and to keep asking yourself questions."

She passed a brand-new notebook to each student and said, "Choose a topic you feel passionate about. Think about why this topic is important to you. Look at all sides of it. What are the good sides and the bad sides? How would others see it? What would you like to change? What do you want others to understand?

"And don't share your journals yet. Keep them to yourselves so that you can write freely, without wondering what others would say. What is important is that you write every day."

Miss Jones asked the students to jot down any thoughts they might have in response to the assignment, and to be sure to add any new questions as they came up.

Their teacher was still talking when the lunch bell rang. Hurriedly she added, "Since I don't know what your topics will be, I can't give you any more directions than to think, think, think, and write, write, write. But once you have begun writing, you can always talk to me."

The students stood up to get in line for lunch.

"So, what's your passion in life?" Camille asked Margie the minute they joined the line.

"I don't know. Whatever," answered Margie. She thought Miss Jones's explanation had taken too long. She wasn't very sure about the assignment and wanted some time to think about it.

Unfazed by Margie's lukewarm response, Camille said, "Mine is dolphins." She said it with such enthusiasm that it caught Margie by surprise.

"Really?" was all she could answer.

"Yes, really," Camille affirmed. "They really are my passion." As she smiled again, Margie found herself smiling back.

# 7. Dolphins Every Day

During the following weeks Margie learned much more about dolphins than she ever thought it was possible to know. Camille was serious about her passion. Fortunately, she was also fun to be with.

"Did you know, Margie," she would begin, and then mention another interesting fact. She knew many things about dolphins in the wild, including that there are more than thirty different species of dolphins, from the huge orcas to the various kinds that are only four feet long. Camille told Margie that the ones most commonly seen in captivity are Atlantic bottlenose dolphins, but that her own favorite was the Commerson's dolphin. One of the smallest species, Commerson's dolphins are very fast swimmers and jump extremely high.

Camille also informed Margie that there are dolphins in every ocean and even in some rivers, including the pink dolphins that live in the Amazon River in South America. Most fascinating of all, she explained that dolphin pods are matriarchal. The leading dolphin is an older female who has had many offspring, while the older males are at the bottom of the social order.

Margie was especially interested to learn how dolphins are born. Since small dolphins are vulnerable to being eaten by sharks, other female dolphins help a mother who is about to give birth by forming a protective circle around her. When the baby dolphin is born, the mother dolphin swims under the newborn to bring her calf to the surface, where it can take its first breaths of air protected by a loving circle of friends.

Camille also knew about dolphins and orcas living in marine-life parks all over the world. She knew the exact water temperature in each of the parks she'd visited, the trainers' routines, and the behaviors that the dolphins were taught to perform.

Margie enjoyed listening to Camille. Her enthusiasm was contagious. And Margie began sharing her own interest in music and books.

One day as they sat chatting in the school cafeteria, Margie started thinking about how different her conversations with Camille were in comparison to her time with Lupe.

Lupe's English was still very limited, as was Margie's Spanish. Each of them knew isolated words and simple sentences they could say to each other. Those words and phrases were enough to navigate the practical moments of the day, but not enough to share their deeper thoughts and feelings, the way she and Camille had begun to do.

*Lupe must have felt so alone when she was in my class,* Margie thought. It was good to know that her cousin seemed to be enjoying the bilingual class. It helped Margie feel less guilty to think that Lupe might have the chance to make some friends of her own.

Meanwhile, John and Peter had given up teasing Margie about Lupe. At first they tried to tease Camille about being taller than everyone in the class, but she just laughed and didn't let it bother her, so they soon stopped. Now they seemed more interested in talking about the performance of their favorite football players than in bothering girls who paid no attention to them.

There was no doubt about what Camille's project would be. She wasn't sure what she would do for her final activity, but some of the questions she was wrestling with included "Should I become a trainer or a marine biologist?" "Should dolphins be bred in captivity, or should they be kept in captivity for a short while only if they are injured, and then released back to the wild as soon as possible?" "Does seeing dolphins at close range in an aquarium really help people become more interested in saving wild dolphins?" and "How can we convince the fishing industry not to kill dolphins with their nets?"

Instead of feeling overwhelmed by all these questions and the different directions that her project might take, Camille just wrote and wrote, filling many pages in her journal. In contrast, Margie had written very little in hers. She had written down a few thoughts, but she was unsure about how to pursue them further. She thought she might write about herself and about how important it was to her to be an American. She knew family was important to her too, and she knew that she wanted to feel good about herself, both at home and at school. She didn't like feeling guilty about some of the ways she had been acting, but she wasn't sure if she could write about that.

She also wished that she didn't feel so embarrassed about Lupe, since after all, there was nothing wrong with her cousin, except that she didn't know English. Yet Lupe's presence still made her feel uncomfortable and tight inside. Margie felt troubled by the thought that she was growing apart from her own family, instead of closer to them.

Margie wished she didn't miss her mother so much, especially since her mother was right there at home. But she did not quite know how to start writing about all of these things.

*My parents feel so Mexican all of a sudden. How can I be as American as I want to be and still feel close to them?* she kept asking herself. Even what it meant to be "American" seemed less clear to her than before, when she had thought it was simply a matter of where you were born or the papers you had.

Finally Margie decided to follow Miss Jones's advice and start writing down some of her questions and ideas. She hoped that by doing so, her thoughts and feelings would stop swimming around in her head and start to become a little clearer.

*I am American!*
*Sometimes I feel like I'm not American*
    *enough.*
*Can Lupe become American someday?*

*Why don't my parents feel American to me?*
*Are they really Mexican even though they*
    *live here now?*
*Do my parents feel closer to Lupe because*
    *she is Mexican like them?*
*I do like Lupe.*
*Sometimes I feel sorry for her.*
*Sometimes I admire her.*
*Sometimes I am jealous of her.*
*Can things be different?*
*How could they change?*

# 8. Library Helpers

On Tuesdays and Thursdays after school Camille stayed with Margie while she waited for Lupe. Many of those afternoons they went to the school library. One day Ms. Faggioni, the librarian, asked them, "Do you girls have permission from home to stay after school? How would you like to be my helpers?"

Before Margie had time to say anything, Camille answered for both of them: "That would be great. And could we look things up on the Internet sometimes? You know, like dolphins?"

The librarian smiled. Camille had already checked out every book on dolphins that the library owned.

From then on they helped the librarian twice a week. They put the returned books back on the shelves where they belonged so that others could easily find them again. Sometimes they would go through whole shelves, checking to see that each book was in the right place.

Though Ms. Faggioni appreciated the girls' help, she also encouraged them to sit and read.

Camille preferred books on nature, particularly those about surviving in the wild. She enjoyed reading about the many months a young boy spent in the wild with his raccoon in *My Side of the Mountain*, about how Julie developed a relationship with wolves in *Julie of the Wolves*, and about the work it took to survive a bitter winter in *Hatchet*. Her favorite was *Island of the Blue Dolphins*. She told Margie she could imagine living alone on an island on the California coast and feeling connected to all the other beings that lived there.

Margie looked for books with a touch of adventure. When she discovered *Salamandastron*, she was fascinated by the world it described, and then read every book in the Redwall series, eager to follow the adventures of the small animals living in Redwall Abbey as they escaped from the nasty foxes and vixens.

"Don't you find many of those words hard to understand?" Camille asked her one afternoon, pointing to the page Margie was reading.

"Yes, but I like looking them up. The dictionary and I are old friends," Margie replied.

Margie had become comfortable with the dictionary early on. When she realized there were many English words that her mother could not explain to her, and since her father was not usually back from work when Margie came home from school, Margie asked her parents for a dictionary. At first her father bought her a pocket dictionary, but the type was so small it was hard to find the words. When Margie explained the difficulty, he got her a much larger desk edition. Once Margie got used to looking up words, she discovered that she really enjoyed doing so, and she began searching for new words to look up. It became almost like a game for her, a treasure hunt where every new word she found was a jewel to store away, something of value that she might use someday.

"I've never known anyone who enjoyed looking things up in the dictionary," Camille said. "But I love looking things up on the Internet, so I think I understand."

Margie smiled. She could not remember the last time she'd had so much fun with a friend. They began to stay later and later at the library each week, until finally Lupe had to start coming to get Margie when *baile folklórico* practice was over.

The first few times that Lupe showed up at the

door of the library with her face all bright and glowing from dance practice, Margie quickly said goodbye to Camille and rushed out, ready to go home. She didn't want to have to feel ashamed of Lupe in front of Camille.

But one day, before Margie was able to say goodbye, Camille greeted her cousin with a smile, saying, "Hi there, Lupe."

Lupe was caught by surprise by Camille's friendly greeting. Embarrassed, she looked down and said nothing.

Before Lupe could recover and say hello, Margie grabbed her arm and led her out of the library. Margie walked straight home, with Lupe tagging silently behind.

Lupe tried to understand what was happening. Was her cousin ashamed of her because she didn't speak English? Or was it because Lupe didn't have a home of her own and had to live at Margie's?

Lupe's greatest fear was that Margie might resent having to share her home and her parents with her Mexican cousin. Just a few days ago Mrs. Rodríguez had told her class that in order to understand someone, it was important to imagine what it might be like to "walk in that person's shoes."

Now Lupe wondered how it would feel to be in Margie's shoes. She wanted to think that if she were the one with a nice house and two parents who lived together, she would be happy to have her cousin come and live with her. But how could she be so sure?

No matter how hard Lupe thought about it, nothing seemed to ease the worry she felt during that long walk home.

# 9. Christmas or Navidad?

Christmas had always been Margie's favorite time of year. She loved everything about it: the outdoor lights decorating the streets, the Christmas carols on the radio, the colorful paper used for wrapping gifts. She especially loved going with her parents to find a tree and talking her father into buying the tallest one that would still fit inside their family room.

Christmas made Margie feel more American than ever. Even if her mother sometimes softly sang songs of her own or had the radio on a Spanish station, Margie could still sing "Rudolph the Red-Nosed Reindeer" or "Santa Claus Is Coming to Town" at the top of her lungs. She also liked singing "Silent Night" to herself while going to sleep. Each of those songs felt like a treasure to her. And like any treasure, she'd had to work hard for them.

Margie remembered a time when she did not

know any of those songs, yet all the other children sang them so easily.

"We don't have a Christmas tree like everyone else does!" she had wailed to her mother. "And why do you always have the radio on in Spanish? How am I going to learn the songs that everyone else knows?"

Her mother was so upset that she cried. It was the first time Margie had seen her mother cry, and she felt really bad.

But her father took her to buy a tree, a little tree that first time. And her mother bought ornaments. A few days later, on Christmas Day, Margie found a box with a small CD player and two CDs with Christmas carols under the tree. She played them for months, long after everyone else had stopped thinking about that Christmas past, and long before they started planning for the next one still to come. And when Christmas finally came around again, Margie could sing along with most of the carols the others sang, even though some of the words didn't mean much to her, such as "Deck the halls with boughs of holly."

Those songs had become her own—to know, to share, to prove that she belonged. And now, having taken the time to look up anything she did not know, she understood every word.

Something else Margie liked about Christmas was that her father was often able to take a few days' vacation. They would do special things, such as drive down to San Francisco to see the big tree in Union Square, the festive window displays downtown, and the beautifully decorated houses. Last year they had even gone ice-skating at the rink in Embarcadero Center.

Above all, Christmas gave Margie a sense of belonging. Somehow she felt that by encouraging her parents to celebrate Christmas the American way, she was helping them to become more American.

But this Christmas with Lupe was already turning out to be quite different. "We must make Lupe feel at home. It's hard being away from home at Christmastime," Margie's mother had said. Though that sounded very nice, it turned out to mean more changes than Margie had anticipated. Now her parents could not stop reminiscing about their own childhood Christmas seasons in Mexico, which they called *Navidades*. Her mother kept playing *villancicos,* Spanish Christmas carols, and encouraging Lupe to sing along. And the house seemed to be continuously filled with visitors who spoke endearingly in Spanish to the girls. But Margie thought they talked too fast, and she could hardly understand a word they said.

Yet none of this was as awful as realizing that her parents were planning to have a *nacimiento*, a Nativity scene, this year instead of a Christmas tree.

"*¡Ya verás qué lindo!* You'll see! It will be wonderful," Margie's mother tried to tell her. But when Margie saw the pile of grocery boxes covered with brown butcher paper in the corner of the family room where the brightly lit tree had always stood, she said angrily, "It won't be Christmas without a tree." She stormed off to her room and shut the door so that she could be alone.

The next day Margie woke up to the smell of *chocolate caliente* and *churros*. She stretched in bed for a moment and then threw on a pair of jeans and a turtleneck before rushing downstairs.

"*Churros y chocolate* is the best alarm clock I've ever found," said her father as he set a plate of *churros* on the table.

The radio was playing "Feliz Navidad," and her mother had set the table with the embroidered tablecloth that Lupe had brought as a present from Tía Dolores. As a centerpiece she had filled a large ceramic pot with calla lilies.

"Looks like Diego Rivera, right?" Lupe asked Margie. Although Lupe always spoke in Spanish to Margie's parents, she made a point of speaking to Margie in English.

Margie looked at Lupe and shrugged. She had no idea what Lupe was talking about.

Lupe left the table and dashed out of the dining room.

"What's going on, Margie?" her mother asked with a note of concern in her voice.

"I don't know," said Margie. She wanted to start eating the *churros*, but she was worried about her cousin. It wasn't like Lupe to just leave the room like that.

Then Lupe was back, bringing a book with her to show everyone a picture of a famous painting by Diego Rivera—a large clay pot filled with white calla lilies. Lupe's eyes sparkled with pride and joy.

Margie looked at her mother's table decoration and then at the picture in the book. The painting had such deep and powerful hues! Margie was surprised to see how the painter had turned something so common into such a work of art. She had often seen Lupe looking at that book. No wonder Lupe liked it so much!

While Margie helped clean the table and do the dishes, she was lost in thought. Since Diego Rivera was a Mexican painter, maybe he made Lupe feel proud to be Mexican. Margie was so used to thinking about Mexico as a very poor place, where people had all kinds of problems, a place that no one would feel proud of having as their birthplace. Now she had something new to think about.

The moment they finished putting away the dishes, Lupe pleaded, "Come, Margarita, let's make the *nacimiento* really pretty!"

With the taste of *churros y chocolate* still lingering in her mouth, Margie followed her cousin to the family room.

The boxes covered with butcher paper were beginning to look like a desert landscape. Margie's mother had filled several trays with small jars of sprouted wheat, and her father had brought in a small fan. Its gentle breeze moved over the tender green wheat fields, bringing the scene to life.

"Don't you like it?" Lupe asked. "Do you want us to have a lake? We can make one, with a mirror. And a river . . . we can make one with . . . with . . . *papel de aluminio.*"

"Aluminum foil," said Margie helpfully. She had

not heard Lupe string together so many words in English before. "Sure! Let's do it!" she replied.

The girls placed and replaced the little houses, changing the scene again and again. They tried putting the shepherds and their sheep in a canyon made from creased butcher paper, only to take them down later and move them to a different spot.

Finding a special place for the three wise men was the most challenging part of all. Lupe called them *los Reyes Magos* and talked about them as if they were personal friends. "This is Melchor," she said to Margie, showing her the one who looked to be the oldest and rode a camel. "He comes from Arabia." Then she added, "And this is Gaspar, the youngest one, who rode his horse all the way from Persia."

Margie began seeing the figures differently now that she knew they had names.

"Which is your favorite?" asked Lupe. Without waiting for an answer, she added, "My favorite is Baltasar, who came from Africa riding on an elephant. I'd love to ride an elephant too someday!"

They worked together for several hours without noticing how much time had gone by. If they were not going to have a tree this year, Margie was determined that this *nacimiento* would be as beautiful as possible.

As Margie worked on this new project, she felt all mixed up inside. Her special Christmastime had changed. It was not just her and her parents anymore. This Christmas was very different from all the previous ones, and she felt a loss. Yet having her cousin as part of the family meant that they were spending more time together during the holidays. And almost despite herself, Margie was enjoying some of the new things she was learning.

Maybe there was enough room at Christmas for calla lilies as well as poinsettias.

Then Margie did something that seemed very natural to Lupe, although it had never felt natural to Margie before. After giving each of her parents a big hug and kiss, Margie gave her cousin a big hug too.

# 10. True Christmas Gifts

This first Christmas in the United States, away from Mexico and everything she had always known, felt very special to Lupe. There were many things she missed in a way she could hardly begin to explain: At home a certain atmosphere pervaded the town, a combination of many small details, even a different smell in the air always accompanied this joyful time of year.

Some of the things she missed were easier to name, such as *La pastorela*, an old traditional play about the shepherds who were told that a special baby had been born in a manger. The townspeople performed this play every year at Christmastime, and Lupe never grew tired of seeing it.

There was also the big celebration in the plaza, where the *danzantes*, dressed in their colorful costumes and wearing large feather crowns, would dance for hours. Most of all, there was the feeling of anticipation, the excitement of knowing that something wondrous was about to happen.

On New Year's Eve the fireworks in the plaza illuminated the whole town and left a lingering smell of gunpowder in the air.

Everyone looked forward to *el Día de los Reyes Magos* on January 6, when the three wise men brought the children their gifts. Like most of her friends, Lupe did not expect to receive many elaborate toys as presents, since few people could afford that. But whatever gifts they received on the morning of the sixth brought much joy and led to a great deal of play and laughter for many days afterward.

Like everything else she was experiencing here, Christmas in California was very different.

A few days before Christmas, Margie was impatiently going through her CDs, looking for a specific Christmas carol.

"I can't wait to have an iPod," she said. "I hope Santa will bring me one. These CDs are so ridiculous."

Lupe was silent. She could not believe her cousin. She had been admiring the fact that Margie owned so many CDs. Margie played them on a small boom box the family had in the dining room. It was very handy and had a pair of headphones so that Margie could listen to whatever music she liked.

Sometimes Margie would take out the headphones so that Lupe could hear also. Lupe always enjoyed it immensely when Margie played her music for both of them.

Lupe was surprised at the way Margie would constantly skip songs and change CDs. She would have preferred to hear each song all the way through until it finished. Just as Lupe was starting to understand some of the words in the song, Margie would skip to the next one or open the player to switch discs. Whenever a song was playing, Margie was already looking for the next CD she wanted to hear.

Now, as she looked at the CD player, Lupe thought, *Yes, that's how I feel in this country, always fast-forwarded. The minute I think I have caught up with things, it turns out that I need to learn something new.*

Having to be constantly moving forward, faster than she could take in all of the new experiences coming her way, was not a good feeling. Yet Lupe smiled. Even bad feelings got better when you understood where they were coming from. Doing a takeoff on the introductions that they had role-played in her

ESL class, Lupe thought, *Hi, I'm Lupe, the CD player in fast-forward mode, with the disc being changed constantly.*

On Christmas morning it was hard for Margie to hide her disappointment when she did not receive an iPod. There were many other presents: a new backpack, a sweater she had admired the day she accompanied her mother to the mall, and a pair of Rollerblades. She made an effort to be grateful and to look as happy as she knew her parents wanted her to be.

Each time Lupe opened a package, she gasped with delight. "This is the most wonderful present ever!" Lupe said excitedly when she unwrapped a wooden artist's box filled with brushes, paints, and a palette. Even though Lupe spoke in Spanish, Margie had no problem understanding her cousin's great joy.

Margie had been thinking that it was probably Lupe's fault that she had not gotten her iPod. Her parents had always gone to great lengths to get her what she most wanted. But now, since they had to buy presents for two girls, it would naturally be harder for them to do so.

Yet when Margie looked at Lupe and saw the excitement on her cousin's face, suddenly the iPod did not seem so important anymore.

Later that day, when Lupe asked her to sit still so that she could draw her portrait, Margie said, "Sure. But first let me find us some good music to listen to." She placed a CD in the player and let it play all the way through while she posed for Lupe.

# 11. Trainers for a Day

The first day after Christmas vacation, when Margie and Camille entered the library and saw the huge pile of books that had been returned, they both said, "Oh, my!" Yet they felt more excited than worried, as they liked their work and knew they were being useful. They took off their sweaters and got down to business.

Margie could not believe how tan Camille was and how much lighter her hair had become.

"We went to Florida to visit my grandmother, and then we went to the Keys," explained Camille while they were sorting through the mountain of books. "We swam with dolphins and were trainers for a day," Camille added.

"Trainers for a day?"

"Yes. You get to spend a day—well, it's more like a morning—at a marine-life park where they have dolphins and sea lions. And the trainers teach you how to give the animals commands to do certain things, like vocalize, splash water at you, and even give you a kiss. Then you get to give them commands and have the animals respond, just like if you were their trainer."

"Really? You got to do all that?"

"Yeah. And then they show you how to prepare food for each animal. They have this big kitchen with a huge refrigerator where the fish is kept, and everything is very, very clean. You have to wash your hands like a surgeon does, to make sure there are no bacteria that could make the animals sick. There is a chart with the name and weight of each dolphin and sea lion, and next to each name it shows how many pounds of food the animal needs to eat, according to its weight, for each meal of the day. And the fish and squid that they feed the animals is all really fresh, restaurant quality."

"Yuck! I don't like fish. But wow, you are really lucky!"

"And so are you. Because my dad said you should get your parents' permission to come with us to Discovery Kingdom in Vallejo this Sunday. My parents are taking my sisters, Jessica and Collette, and me. Since I've been there so many times, I know some of the trainers, and we'll get to talk to them between shows."

"Do you really mean it?" Margie was having trouble accepting all this. With her blond hair and her tan in the middle of the winter, Camille almost looked like a trainer herself. And she wanted to take Margie to a marine-life park!

Suddenly she remembered Lupe, and her excitement quickly faded. "Well, I'm not sure. I really want to go, but my mom . . . I know my mom . . ." She wanted to say that her mom would want her to bring Lupe, but she couldn't.

"You can talk her into it. And you can bring your cousin, too."

"Really?" The excitement returned so fast Margie felt as though she had just been zapped by lightning. "Lupe?" Margie couldn't believe that the invitation would include Lupe. Why would Camille want to bring Lupe? "But . . . she can hardly speak English."

"That's okay. I knew you'd want to bring her, so I asked my parents if you could both come. She's always so quiet, but I bet you she'll love the dolphins too. And don't worry. My dad speaks Spanish. He'll talk to her. Maybe I can start speaking some

Spanish too. I'm getting tired of going to Florida and not understanding half of my relatives."

"Your relatives speak Spanish? How come? You're not . . ." Suddenly Margie felt very stupid.

"Well, at least half of them do. All of my dad's family does. My *bisabuela* in Florida and my grandmother are Cuban, and my grandfather is from Peru," explained Camille matter-of-factly.

Margie looked at Camille as if she had never seen her before. This tall blond girl, with such fair skin and no accent, had a Latino father. There was no question she was American, but she didn't seem to mind that her relatives were not.

"And here I thought you were so totally American," Margie replied, completely surprised.

"That's funny, so did I," said Camille, laughing. "I *am* American, and I'm the same person you knew before you found out that half of my family comes from other countries." Smiling at Margie, she added, "Haven't you figured it out yet? The United States is made up of all different kinds of people. And most of their ancestors came here from other places, even though they may have forgotten about it or may be trying to pretend that their family has always been here. The only people who have always been here are the Native Americans! And there is more Native American in your Mexican family and in my Peruvian family than in most people's families, including those people who pretend that they belong here and other people don't."

"Why didn't you tell me about your family?" Margie asked, still feeling more than a little confused by everything her friend was saying.

"I don't know . . . maybe because it doesn't matter to me where my family is from. Well, I don't mean it that way. Perhaps the real reason is that I'm kind of embarrassed about not speaking Spanish. I don't know why they didn't teach me when I was little, but now it's not so easy to learn."

*Now, that sounds to me like being embarrassed for all the wrong reasons!* Margie thought.

Margie didn't know what to make of everything. Miss Jones kept saying that writing helped to clarify one's thoughts. Maybe this was something she could be writing about in her journal. She would write the question "What does it really mean to be an American?" and search for the answers.

Lupe came into the library from dance practice with her cheeks bright red and her forehead still covered with sweat. She stopped at the door, as if she did not want to interrupt.

*"Hola, Lupe, ¿cómo estás?"* said Camille, practicing some of the phrases she had been using in Florida.

Lupe smiled at her but didn't say anything.

As Camille began putting on her sweater, she said, "Margie, don't forget to ask your parents if you and Lupe can come to Discovery Kingdom, and maybe even spend the night at my house."

Lupe could not believe her ears. She was delighted to be included but decided to wait until later to ask Margie any questions and have her clarify whether this wonderful invitation was really true.

Meanwhile, Margie was shaking her head at her friend Camille, as if to say, *I can't believe you never told me half of your family speaks Spanish.* As though she were reading Margie's mind, Camille smiled at her and said, "My father says all the time, 'What's important is what you learn after you already think that you know everything.' See you tomorrow!"

# 12. Riding an Elephant

That weekend the trip to the marine-life park turned out to be everything Margie could have possibly wanted, and more. Camille's parents were enthusiastic about dolphins and the marine park. Jessica and Lupe hit it off right away, and made friends easily without much need for words. Camille's youngest sister, Collette, loved the animals, and her parents enjoyed watching her animated responses. The family had obviously been to the park many times before and knew the schedules for the different shows and what to expect at each one.

Camille's father spoke in Spanish with Lupe, and they laughed just as Lupe did with Margie's parents. Camille and Jessica attempted to say a few phrases in Spanish, and for once Margie did not feel embarrassed about her home language. She joined in, and although she was not fluent, she was proud that her pronunciation sounded like that of a native speaker.

When Lupe said something to Camille's father about the *nacimiento* they had built at Margie's house, he told them that when he was a young boy, his family had celebrated both Christmas and January 6, *el Día de los Reyes Magos.* "We were the only kids in the neighborhood who got presents twice! By the time we were tired of playing with our Christmas toys, it was time for a whole new set of gifts," he told them. Then he laughed and said, "Not that we ever really got tired of playing with any of our toys, since they were always things we could build on and add to. We had train sets and car tracks going all over the house, from room to room, and we built towns and farms all around those tracks. I'm afraid our house looked more like a playground than a house!" Margie thought that getting two sets of presents was not a bad idea at all.

At times during the day Camille and Margie would walk on ahead, and they even got to see a few shows together without the rest of the crew. At other times the four older girls went on some of the bigger rides, while Camille's parents and Collette waited for them to finish. Afterward they would all come back together as a group.

Seeing the dolphins, Margie understood why

Camille loved them so much. These majestic creatures seemed to glide through the water, as well as fly through the air whenever they leaped up to do their tricks. The dolphins played with one another and even interacted with Camille through the window. Camille could spend hours playing with them—putting her face up next to the glass, showing the dolphins a stuffed animal and moving it around from window to window, playing tag with the dolphins.

Margie enjoyed listening to Camille ask the trainers all kinds of questions, and was delighted when they included her in the conversation. But the best part for Margie was feeling so at ease with Camille and her family and not feeling embarrassed about Lupe.

Before, Margie had worried so much that if she got too close to Lupe, others might start teasing her or making fun of her again. And now here was Camille, the girl she admired so much, sharing a chocolate bar and giggling with Lupe as if she had known her all her life.

Camille saw Margie looking at her and Lupe and asked, "What are you thinking about?"

"Nothing," Margie lied.

"All right. Let's all go see the orca show!" Camille

suggested with a smile. "Dad, we will meet you at seven thirty at the front gate of Merlin's Island Party. Okay?"

"Be careful . . . ," he called after them as the four girls ran toward the stadium where the beautiful orcas and their trainers would be performing.

The music was loud and animated. Margie saw everyone clapping and moving to the beat. *People from all over come to see these beautiful creatures and to enjoy the show,* she thought. As she looked around and noticed the different people in the audience, she wondered, *How many different countries do they come from? How many different languages do they speak? I hope that someday I get to visit their countries and hear their languages, even if I don't understand them. Yet right now there is nothing between us that feels foreign or strange; we are all just people enjoying the show together.*

Just then the trainer reemerged from the water, standing tall on the orca's head, and Margie let out a big sigh. Yet her relief had as much to do with the thoughts that were swimming around inside her head as with the rousing finale to the performance.

*   *   *

When the show was over, they headed toward the gate. As Margie walked slowly through the crowd, her mind drifted back over the day, savoring all she had experienced.

For the first time since Lupe had come to live with them, Margie felt truly happy. The constant worry that had been wearing away at her was gone. It seemed like it had been a good day for everyone else, too.

Margie felt especially happy knowing that even Lupe's wildest dream had now come true—she had gotten to ride an elephant!

When the whole crew had gone to see the large land animals—the white tigers, the tall giraffes, and the Asian elephants—Camille's father had noticed how fascinated Lupe was by the elephants and suggested that she might want to ride one. A moment later he had bought her a ticket.

Lupe also got to feed the elephants and play tug-of-war with them, but it was clear to Margie that getting to ride an elephant had been the most exciting part of the day for Lupe.

"I've always thought that of the three wise men

Baltasar is the one who brought me presents on *el Día de los Reyes*. And now I've gotten to ride an elephant just like his!" Lupe cried. *"¡Qué elefante tan maravilloso!* Wasn't the elephant so graceful and strong?" she kept repeating.

"It's strange," Margie said to Camille. "When she's happy, it's like English just bursts out of her mouth. But when she is worried, she can't figure out how to say the simplest thing."

"I don't think that's so strange," said Camille. "I used to sing really loud in the shower or when I was all by myself, but whenever someone was watching, my voice seemed to go all wrong. Now that I'm in choir, I really love to sing, even when I'm in front of a group of people. It's almost my favorite thing now."

"Yeah, I bet I can guess what your most favorite thing is!" said Margie, pointing to the tank where the dolphins were frolicking.

Both girls laughed. Then Margie added, "Now I have one more thing to write down in my journal: 'Being happy helps people learn languages and do other things better.'"

They returned home late, ready for a shower and bed. While taking her shower, Margie kept thinking about her day. So many new and wonderful things!

It had been good to see Lupe happy for a whole day. Being far away from home must be really hard for her, even though she never complained. Watching Lupe laugh so easily as she sat on top of the elephant, Margie had realized how brave her cousin really was.

The dolphin and whale shows had been amazing too. Seeing the young female trainer swim around in the tank with the dolphins had been breathtaking.

And how different it was to see some things through the eyes of others. It was amazing to hear Camille say, "What beautiful hair you have, Lupe. It's like my *tía* Rosa's. I've always wanted to have long black hair like that!"

# 13. Finding Answers

The Monday after the visit to the marine-life park, Mrs. Rodríguez was absent and there was a substitute teacher in Lupe's class. "We will be going to the library so that each of you can get a book. You will have one hour to read the book, and later you will share what you have read with the class," she told them.

Lupe immediately chose a book about elephants. Until her day at Discovery Kingdom, elephants—giant animals such as the one that *el rey* Baltasar rode—had been mythical creatures to her. But now, having ridden one herself and having observed them up close, she was intrigued and full of questions. How long could an elephant live? How long did mother elephants carry their unborn baby elephants? How long did it take for a baby elephant to grow? What did they eat in the wild? Was it true that elephants have amazing memories? Which elephant led the herd?

As they walked back to class, Lupe wrapped

both arms around the large book with magnificent elephant photos and held it close to her heart. She could not wait to read it.

Once she began looking through the book, she started picturing herself riding the elephant again. What an incredible experience that had been! She had never before dared to imagine that one day she would get to do that.

It had been a real treat to spend time with Camille's family. She'd especially enjoyed meeting Jessica, who'd been so friendly to her and so much fun.

Lupe had noticed with admiration that Jessica carried a sketch pad and coloring pencils with her in a large bag, and that she'd stop from time to time to sketch what she saw. She looked very absorbed in her drawing and seemed to enjoy it so much that she didn't care about what others might think. *She loves drawing as much as I do,* thought Lupe, realizing that she, too, could carry her drawing materials with her and feel equally at ease.

Jessica had also promised that the two of them would go someday to visit the Academy of Sciences. After the elephant ride she'd started to tell Lupe about her own favorite animals:

"I saw them for the first time at the Academy of Sciences. Though they're not big, like dolphins or elephants, they are really magical."

Filled with curiosity, Lupe asked, "What are they?"

Lowering her voice, as if to share a great secret, Jessica answered, "Sea dragons."

"Sea dragons?" Lupe was disappointed. "I thought you meant real animals. Sea dragons are fantasy."

"But they *are* real . . . wait until you see them! They are just adorable." And flashing her engaging smile, she added, "I know you'll agree that there is nothing else like them in the whole wide world."

"What do they look like?" Lupe asked.

Sighing with longing, Jessica explained, "They're animals, like sea horses, only larger. But when you see them, they look a little like plants. Their wings—because they do have wings—look like branches or algae, and when they move in the water, it looks like they are flying. You have to see them to believe it. They are *so beautiful!*"

Lupe was very much looking forward to visiting these extraordinary creatures from the Australian ocean, but she wasn't sure what she was looking forward to more: seeing the magical sea dragons or spending more time with Jessica.

Lupe tried to imagine what it might be like to be part of a family like Jessica's, with both a mother and a father who were able to stay together. As wonderful as the day had been, she didn't think she'd need to visit a park to be happy. Just being together would be enough.

Lupe felt the old familiar pain that was connected to her father's disappearance and her mother's sadness. She hid her face in the elephant book and blinked quickly to hold back the tears, but she still had to wipe her eyes with the back of her hand.

Then the image of Tía Consuelo came to mind. She would have been upset to know that Lupe was so sad. Even if her aunt and uncle were not her real parents, they had welcomed her with great kindness. She could tell that her presence meant something special to her aunt, a connection to the brother she had lost; and her uncle, although not related to her by blood, was always generous with her. Perhaps she reminded Tío Francisco of what his wife, Consuelo, might have been like as a child.

Yesterday at the park it seemed that Margie was finally feeling more comfortable sharing her friends with Lupe. The friendship with her cousin that had started to grow during Christmas vacation had felt precarious at first, but now it looked as though it might be here to stay.

Lupe sighed one of those deep sighs that always prompted her aunt to give her a big hug. But her aunt was not there, and so Lupe wrapped her arms around herself and gave herself a little squeeze. Then she smiled and went back to reading her book, to see if she could find the information she wanted— although answers to questions about elephants were much easier to find than answers to questions about her own life.

# 14. Folklórico Dance

On Tuesday when Margie came out of class, Lupe was waiting for her right outside the classroom. She stood shyly against the wall in the hallway.

"There is your cousin, Margareeeta," John taunted.

"Can she speak English yet?" Peter added.

"She's smarter than the two of you put together," said Camille as she straightened up to look even taller.

The boys left, laughing but without saying anything else.

"Hi, Margie. *Hola*, Camille. Margie, Mrs. Rodríguez wants you to come," Lupe said in her slow, heavily accented English.

"Me? Why?" Margie was worried. Was Lupe in trouble?

"Nothing is wrong . . . she just wants to see you." When Lupe saw Margie hesitate, she added, "*Ahora mismo, por favor.* She is waiting."

"Okay, Lupe, I'm coming. Camille, I'm not sure what this is all about. If I don't make it to the library, please explain to Ms. Faggioni."

"Sure. Will do," said Camille as she walked toward the library.

Margie followed Lupe to the other side of the school, past the main school yard, to the portables that housed the bilingual classes, the speech therapist, and the special education class.

Mrs. Rodríguez was tall and slender, and her round black eyes seemed to reach right inside Margie's heart.

*"¿Margarita, podrías bailar con nosotros, por favor?"* Her Spanish sounded soft and musical, and Margie was pleased that she had understood.

Dancing was something she truly enjoyed, but she hesitated at first, answering in English, "Dance? Why me?"

"Well, you are the right height, and we need another girl while Vanessa gets over the flu. Since you are going to be waiting for Lupe anyway, would you mind terribly?"

"I guess it would be okay," said Margie, "if it's only for a few days. But I really don't know how to dance anything Mexican."

"You'll learn. I'm sure you'll be fine."

One hour later Margie was not so sure at all. This Mexican *folklórico* dance was not like anything she had ever danced before.

When Margie was younger, her father would often find a Sunday evening program of dance music on the radio, and take turns dancing soft boleros and lively salsa with Margie and her mother. The few times she had been able to visit Liz, they had listened to pop songs and had a fun time making up their own dance moves. But these dances were another story altogether.

Everyone else seemed to have a clear image of how the dance should look, but all Margie could see were complicated steps, and boys and girls changing places in the wide space left open in the middle of the classroom after all the desks had been pushed back against the wall. Margie was relieved when Mrs. Rodríguez said it was time to go home, but also a little sad, because while she didn't quite have it yet, she had almost finished learning the last step of the dance.

That Thursday and the following Tuesday, Margie crossed the yard gladly after class to join the group in the portable. As the steps became more and more familiar, she started to lose herself in the joy of the music.

Yet on the following Thursday, when she arrived for her fourth practice session, another girl was already there. "This is Vanessa," said Mrs. Rodríguez. "She has come back." Then she added, "But Lucy is absent today, so why don't you stay? You can be our understudy. That way, if we are ever missing a dancer, you can fill in for them."

Margie had never heard the word "understudy" before, and she wasn't sure she liked how it sounded. She would be sure to look it up in the dictionary when she got home. But in the meantime, she was dancing. And as long as she could dance one more day, who cared what it was called?

# 15. Spring Days

Margie loved the way the air smelled in the spring, as well as the anticipation she felt all around her. Two small birds had made their nest in the ivy on the front porch, and her mother had asked everyone to use the back door, so as not to disturb them.

For Margie this meant walking around from the back door to the front of the house several times a day to check on the birds. She agreed that it was important not to disturb them by opening the front door, but at the same time, she needed to know how they were doing.

On those brief outdoor journeys through the overgrowth that filled the narrow space between their house and the house next door, Margie discovered all kinds of wonders: velvety toadstool mushrooms, purple flowers of blossoming clover, a tender fern in the shady spot under the fragrant lilac bush. This world reminded her of the Redwall Abbey series she was reading. A wide variety of animal characters—badgers, squirrels, mice, otters, hares—all planted their vegetable gardens in the land surrounding the abbey. As they gathered nuts and berries among the trees, they were always on the lookout for the menacing foxes and vixens, and taking refuge when needed behind the strong walls of the abbey.

Margie often stopped along the path and got lost in her thoughts. She found herself standing silently, almost as if expecting that one of these animals might appear at any moment. When she heard bees buzzing around the lilacs or glimpsed a darting dragonfly, she let out a sigh. How many treasures might be hidden right here in her own yard?

Maybe this was what she'd write about in her journal. She had written down a few ideas, but she still felt like she had not found something about which she could speak clearly and convincingly to the class.

Margie did not notice that her mother had followed her outside until she felt her mother's arm around her shoulders.

"*Te gustan las flores tanto como a mí*, you like flowers as much as I do," her mother said, smiling. "That's why I gave you a flower name, Margarita. Daisies are so precious. They are such happy flowers, with their bright golden centers. They have always been my favorite. Just like you!"

"Am I really your favorite?"

"*Lo sabes bien, hijita.* You know that very well. My first and only daughter, my most precious girl ever."

Her mother looked into Margie's eyes, and after a pause she asked, "You are not upset that Lupe is here, are you?"

Margie looked around and took a deep breath of the fresh spring air, filled with the fragrance of lilacs. If her mother had asked her this a few months ago, she might have answered differently, but now, no, she was no longer upset that Lupe was here.

"Mami, I love Lupe," she began. And then, not wanting to let this opportunity go by, she added, "Well, I feel that way now. At first I was embarrassed by her, and it bothered me to be seen with her at school. But now I think she is very brave. And I want her to be happy. Have you noticed how she speaks better English when she is happy?"

"Yes, *corazón*, I understand very well that every-thing is easier when one is happy." Margie's mother's arms held her in a warm embrace.

At dinnertime Margie's father brought a large bou-quet of daisies for Margie's mother.

"I couldn't resist, knowing how much you like them," he said, following his words with a kiss.

Margie was pleased. It was nice to see her parents appreciating each other. She had been reading *How Tía Lola Came to (Visit) Stay*, which Ms. Faggioni had recommended to her, and she was realizing more about how difficult things can be when your parents decide that they can't live together any-more. Margie smiled and said, "Daddy, you are so nice."

Lupe brought out a vase, and while Margie's mother placed the daisies on the table, Lupe asked Margie, "Why do you let people call you Margie? You have such a beautiful name. Not just because of the flowers, but also because of the poem."

"The poem? What poem?" asked Margie, intrigued.

"Rubén Darío's poem about the king who had a palace made of diamonds and an entire herd of elephants."

Margie smiled. Lupe's love of elephants was like Camille's love of dolphins.

When Lupe realized Margie did not know what she meant, she continued, "You know, the little princess who went up to the heavens, all the way to the moon and beyond, to pick a star. Rubén Darío wrote this beautiful poem for a girl called Margarita. Even the poem is called 'To Margarita'!"

"People don't know how to pronounce it; not even the teachers say it right . . . and the other kids tease me." Margie heard herself repeating the same explanation she had given her parents many times before, but there was not much conviction left in her voice.

"Well, you can teach the teachers," said Lupe. "After all, some of us have to learn a whole new language. I'm sure they can manage to learn to say our names. And the kids—you can do like Camille does and just laugh."

Margie looked at the flowers and didn't say anything. What was the name of that poet again? A diamond palace and a princess who picked a star as though it were a flower . . . she'd have to ask Ms. Faggioni to help her find that poem. After all, it had been named for her!

# 16. Another Surprise

"Mami, there's a man on the phone asking for you *en español.*"

Margie's mother was taking a tray of enchiladas out of the oven, so she responded, *"¿Quién es, m'hijita?"*

Before Lupe came to live with them, her mother might have said, "Who is it, sweetheart?" But now that Spanish was being used more frequently around the house, Margie's mother was addressing her more and more in Spanish, and her endearing words—*corazón, cariño,* and *hijita*—had reappeared when speaking to her. Margie, feeling proud that she had understood, answered, *"No sé.* I'll ask him."

But when Margie asked the man his name, he hung up.

*"Colgó, Mami,"* Margie explained. "He hung up."

Somehow Margie felt that the call had been important. There had been a sense of urgency in the man's voice. After they finished eating supper, the phone rang again and Margie ran to answer.

This time when the same voice asked for her mother, she said, *"Un momento, por favor. No colgar."* She felt foolish, as she knew she had not said it quite right. She should have said *"No cuelgue,"* but at the moment she had not been able to think of the right form. Well, at least she'd tried.

When her mother picked up the phone and started talking with the man, Margie felt she had helped a little. Even if her Spanish had been awkward, the man had understood.

It had to be important. Her mother took the cordless phone and walked outside to the backyard to carry on the conversation. When she returned, she had a very serious expression on her face. Margie saw a look of understanding pass between her parents.

"Who was it?" asked Margie. Her parents' sharp look told her she should not have asked. Her mother reminded the girls that it was time to do their homework.

The next day Mrs. Rodríguez told the *folklórico* group that there would be no dance practice that afternoon because she had to take one of her sons to the doctor.

When Margie and Lupe returned home from school, there was a strange man sitting in the family room. One of the man's legs was in a cast.

Margie looked at Lupe and realized that her cousin was as surprised as she was. Just at that moment Margie's mother walked in carrying a tray.

"You girls are home early," she said.

"And you didn't go to your class at the community college?" Margie responded with her own question.

After the New Year holidays were over, Margie's mother had registered for a few courses at the community college. "If Lupe is learning English, maybe I can be learning something too," she had explained to the girls. "I would like to be able to help you more with your homework."

She had never missed a class before, so Margie's question was understandable.

But the man frowned at them.

"Come with me, girls," Margie's mother said, putting an arm around each of them and directing them toward the dining room. "I'm sorry. I did not expect you back so early. I was going to wait for you outside."

"¿*Qué pasa, Mami?* Why are you so upset? Who is that man?" Margie rattled off one question after another.

"Lupe, you haven't recognized him? It's my brother, Juan. Your father, Lupe. Your father . . ."

Then, still with an arm around each girl, she walked them to the table.

"Here, let's sit down a moment."

Margie looked at Lupe and saw that her cousin seemed very distant, as if something inside her had suddenly flown away.

Lupe had often dreamed about meeting her father again. Even though her aunt had told her over and over that she should not keep her hopes up, that if her father wanted to find them, he could easily choose to do so, she had never ceased fantasizing about how that moment might feel.

In her dreams her father would appear at the door, playing his guitar and singing in his beautiful voice. He would take her in his arms and lift her high up in the air, as he always used to do. He would smile a gentle smile and tell her how much he had missed her, how much he loved her, and how he would take care of her.

She knew that these daydreams were fantasies, but they had been part of her life for so long that she couldn't imagine living without them.

Any beautiful sight—a bird in flight, the patterns of clouds in the sky—would remind her of her father, make her glad that he had loved her so much, and fill her with hope that he would come find her someday.

A long time ago she had stopped trying to explain her father's absence or come up with stories that might justify his behavior. Instead, she simply held on to her conviction that one day she would see him again.

Now here he was at last, and she had not even recognized him—an overweight man with his leg in a cast and questions in his eyes.

"Do you want to say anything, Lupe? Do you want to ask any questions before you meet him?" Tía Consuelo asked her.

Lupe saw the worried look on her aunt's kind face and asked, "Are you sure it's him, Tía? How did he know where I was?"

*"Ay, hijita,"* was all her aunt could say.

Lupe didn't know what to think or feel, but she did know whom she could hold on to, and so she let herself fall into her aunt's warm embrace.

*     *     *

During the next few days the girls began to learn the story of Juan González.

He had indeed been in Chicago, lured there by some men he had met in Stockton who convinced him that more money could be made working in construction than in the fields. He was there for more than a year, but he did not want to face another Chicago winter, so he moved to Texas.

But Texas was not any easier than the other places where he had worked. Life was difficult for a person without legal status. Many businesses would not hire him, and those that did often paid lower wages. Even though he worked hard, he did not have the rights of other workers. Sometimes the person he worked for would deduct money from his wages for income taxes and Social Security, but no contribution to the government was made in his name. Worse still, he had no medical or disability insurance. He had used most of his savings from the current job to pay for X-rays and to have a doctor put a cast on his leg. He had come to heal at his sister's home because he was out of money.

For days, as he told pieces of his story, it was

clear that it was very painful for him to feel that he barely made enough money and that he was always at risk of being sent back to Mexico. Yet he never said anything about another family. Margie felt that Lupe had the right to know, but she also understood that it was not her place to ask, at least not in front of everyone.

Juan did not speak about any future plans, either. He explained that he had called his sister after he'd had a tractor accident in Napa, not too far from Santa Rosa, where Margie's family lived. Since he needed to stay off that leg for a while, a friend had offered to give him a ride to their home. It all sounded so natural—and it would have been, Margie thought, had he stayed in touch over the years.

Meanwhile, hearing her father go from one story to another, Lupe thought to herself with sadness, *It's almost like when he used to tell us stories in the evenings back home. He's still the hero of every story, but the stories he's telling aren't so nice anymore.*

Both of the girls listened attentively, but neither said a word. Indeed, Juan was the one who did most of the talking.

One thing was clear: Ever since Lupe's father arrived, Francisco and Consuelo had been making an extra effort to be home with the girls as much as they could. Margie felt how they were trying to surround them both with love.

It bothered Margie that Juan would not acknowledge the pain he had caused Lupe for so long. Not that Lupe had ever talked about it, but Margie could feel the pain in her cousin's silence.

One Saturday morning Margie's mother took Lupe to the mall to buy her a new pair of shoes. Margie waited until her father was busy in the yard and then went to the family room and faced Juan.

"*Tu hija . . . muy buena . . . muy buena . . . ,*" she said to her uncle, feeling like never before the need to be able to speak in Spanish. "*Y tú . . . te vas . . . no le dices . . .*"

She burst out crying, whether because of Lupe's pain or her own frustration at not being able to express her feelings, or both, she wasn't sure.

Before she knew it, her own father had his arms around her.

"Here, here, Margarita . . ." His deep and even voice had a calming effect on Margie.

Her father looked at her and at her uncle.

"Why don't you tell me, Margarita, what you are trying to tell your uncle? I'll translate for you."

Margie was not quite sure how to proceed.

"But you won't like me asking him why he has behaved so poorly. I want him to understand that if he leaves again and doesn't tell Lupe where he is going, she is going to be very hurt, just like she was before."

"Well, let me start by telling him what you just said."

Her father began speaking in Spanish to his brother-in-law.

After the two of them had talked for a few minutes, Margie's father squeezed her arm, in a gesture he always used to reassure her.

"I'm glad you have done this, *m'hija*," he said. "*Hablar es bueno*. Things are much better said than held all bottled up inside."

After turning again to say a few words to Lupe's father, he added, "Your uncle's life has not been easy. When men suffer so much, sometimes they forget that the best place to find support is from their families. One mistake can lead to another, and people get used to avoiding the truth. But now your uncle is here, and I think he realizes that he has not been a good father to Lupe. He may not stay around very long. I suspect that now that his leg is better, he'll return soon to the new family he has left behind in Texas. . . ."

Lupe's father seemed to be listening closely to what Margarita's dad was saying. After a moment he nodded and said, *"Sí, sí, Francisco . . . sí, Margarita."*

And then, with a kind expression Margie had not expected to see, he turned to her to thank her for caring for Lupe, saying, *"Gracias por querer a Lupe."*

# 17. Not Your Mistakes

It was a quiet dinner that evening. Ever since Lupe's father had arrived, the girls had not been very talkative over dinner, but today the adults were barely speaking either.

Lupe hardly looked up from her plate, but when she did, she saw her father looking pensively at Margie.

As soon as the meal was over, Lupe's father approached Tío Francisco. The two men spoke briefly for a moment.

Margie's father asked his daughter to help out in the kitchen, while indicating to Lupe that she should join her father in the family room.

Lupe entered the family room slowly. She wanted to spend time with her father, but at the same time she was afraid of the feelings that she struggled with inside. Even the beautiful memories she still carried from bygone days felt dangerous to her. The same painful longings that had nourished all of her fantasies were now fueling her anger against this man who seemed to enter into and disappear from her life so easily.

She stood silently without approaching him, waiting for whatever it was he wanted to say. She refused to give in to the fluttering hope that kept wanting to leap up inside of her.

*"Lupe, hijita . . ."* Her father's voice was surprisingly tender, just as she remembered from years past.

*"Ven, acércate . . . mira."* At his invitation to come closer so that he could show her something, Lupe slowly approached his chair.

*"Es tu hermanita. . . . Se llama Xochitl."* As her father offered her the photo of a little girl, Lupe repeated his words to herself, *My little sister . . . and her name is Xochitl.* She almost missed her father's explanation. "I gave her that name because that's what you used to call your doll. You loved your doll so much. Remember how frightened you were that time you left her behind at your *abuelita*'s house and you thought you had lost her?"

After a pause he added, lowering his voice, almost as if talking to himself and not to Lupe, "I guess I was hoping that someday you might love this little Xochitl as much as you loved your doll Xochitl."

Lupe had not said a word. It was too much to take in at once. She was stunned by the clarity of knowing, beyond the shadow of a doubt, that she had a little sister. She was upset and angry to learn that her father did indeed have another family. At the same time she was also moved, against her will and no matter how much she struggled against it, by the tenderness in his voice as he evoked those long-ago memories that were still so dear to her.

Her father looked at her for a moment and then said, "There is something I must say to you. Please listen. It is important for me, but above all, it is important for you.

"I have behaved poorly, *m'hijita*, very poorly. I have done wrong. It would be fair to say that I have been a bad father and a bad husband. And I am very sorry. Yet my being sorry doesn't change what happened. I never intended for things to turn out the way they have. But what's done can never be undone.

"What is important now is to understand that regardless of what I have done, of the mistakes I made and the pain I have caused you, you do not need to make the same mistakes. You don't.

"You could use my mistakes as an excuse to live your life in anger, to justify anything you choose to do by saying, 'It's because my father abandoned me.' That's what many people do. Find their excuses in the mistakes that others have made. But if you do that, you will gain nothing by it and you'll be wasting your own life.

"Or you could choose to say, 'Something bad happened to me. My father left me and made me suffer very much. But I can make a good life for myself . . . I don't have to continue to suffer for his mistakes.'

"I hope very much, *m'hijita*, that you can do that. Not so much for me, but for your own sake," he finished.

Lupe had listened with her head down, but now she raised her eyes and looked at him.

It seemed to her as though this was the first time she was really seeing her father for who he was. She was seeing him now not as the funny storyteller of her childhood, always the invincible hero in every story, nor as the downcast man who had been staying with them for the last three weeks, the one who kept trying to act as though everything was normal when it wasn't.

Instead, here was someone who was acknowledging his own errors, making a sincere effort to free her from carrying the burden of his own mistakes, and encouraging her to be fully in charge of her own life. Standing before her as a brave and fallible human being, he was doing his best to make amends.

She heard herself saying what Tío Francisco always said, but now the words felt like her own. "It's easy to make mistakes; what's very hard is to admit them."

And then, without a second thought, she gave her father a great big hug.

# 18. Three Families

Saturday mornings were usually slow around the house, but this particular Saturday started off as busy as a regular school day because there was a special rehearsal for the *folklórico* group. Margie and Lupe were so busy helping each other get ready that they did not notice that Lupe's father was in the kitchen making breakfast and the table had already been set.

"What time do you have to be at school for the *folklórico* practice, *m'hija*?" Margie's mother asked her.

"*No sé.* Lupe, what time did Mrs. Rodríguez say *que teníamos que* be there?" As Margie spoke, she poured herself a cup of juice.

"I am not sure, *pero quiero llegar muy* early," responded Lupe as she held out her glass for Margie to fill also.

No one noticed Lupe's father bringing a dish of *huevos rancheros* from the kitchen.

Margie's father entered the room buttoning his shirt and said, "Let's get moving. I need to go to the hardware store before I drop the girls off at school."

*"Buenos días,"* said Juan as he set a basket of warm tortillas and a plate of *pan dulce* on the table.

Everyone stopped as they realized that a breakfast feast had been prepared.

"Let's take a few minutes and sit down," suggested Margie's father. "Girls, Mrs. Rodríguez will understand if you are a little late."

Everyone sat down and helped themselves. No one said much of anything other than *"Por favor . . . gracias"* and *"Muy sabroso"* as the food was being passed around the table.

Then Juan started to speak. *"Francisco, por favor, me traduces,"* he began, asking Francisco to translate.

"I have been thinking a lot lately. I am very grateful for all the love you have given Lupe," Francisco translated. "It is good she is in this country, going to school and learning English.

"I have made many mistakes in the past. However, I now have a house and a family in Texas. And I think Lupe deserves a family of her own." Both Lupe and Margie stopped eating and began listening intently.

*"He decidido que Lupe se merece vivir en Tejas con su nueva familia."*

Before Francisco could translate, both girls cried out at the same time, "No!"

"Lupe belongs *con nosotros*," Margie pleaded.

"I belong . . . here!" Lupe stumbled.

"She is like my sister . . . *como hermana* . . . and she's doing so well in school," Margie explained.

"My English is improving . . . ," Lupe said slowly but clearly.

Both girls were crying and laughing at the same time.

". . . I have friends and the dance," Lupe continued.

"And I don't want her to go," Margie said, continuing to cry.

*"Quiero quedarme con mi tía y mi tío,"* Lupe said, looking at her aunt and uncle.

"I already have a new family . . . here," she said with determination. "*No quiero* . . . I don't want to start over . . . all over again . . . *no quiero pasar por todo eso otra vez."*

"Lupe already has a new life with us," Margie said to all three adults, "and she shouldn't have to leave it!"

"I love you, Papi," Lupe said, "but I would rather live with my new family here."

"We are going to be late . . . we will wait for you in the car," said Margie as she and Lupe walked out the door together.

Margie's parents sat silently, proud that the girls had come together as sisters. They knew that they did not need to translate for Juan what the girls had said, nor their own feelings on the matter.

That afternoon, when Lupe's father announced that he would be returning to Texas the next day, he asked his sister and brother-in-law to please send Lupe to visit him and his family. He showed them pictures of his young wife with Xochitl and Lupe's little brother, a chubby baby boy.

"Lupe needs time to get used to having a third family," Consuelo answered. Putting her arm around Lupe's shoulders, she added, "This is her home now. We are her forever family. Of course, she has her mother and the twins in Mexico, and someday she may want to go see them. Now you are offering that she can also become a part of your new family, where she has a little sister and another baby brother. One day she may discover that having all of these families is indeed a gift, but it may take some time for that to happen."

Margie watched her cousin listening silently to the conversation. What different expressions flew across Lupe's face as she listened to her aunt describing each of her three homes!

"If you ever decide to go, Lupe, and you want me to, I'll go with you. I am your forever sister now." Taking Lupe's hand, Margie pulled her cousin out to the yard, saying, "Come with me. I just learned a new jump-rope song from Camille. Let me teach it to you!"

The girls stayed outside jumping rope for a long time. It felt so good to both of them to jump together in rhythm. Margie could not believe how jealous she had once felt of Lupe, how she had resented having to share her own parents with her and how left out she had felt when they spoke in Spanish.

In turn, Lupe felt amazed at how the distance between her cousin and herself had somehow melted. Perhaps one day she would get to know Xochitl, too, and she would grow to love her. But there was no question that at this moment Margie truly felt like her sister.

While the girls were jumping rope, Margie's father went out on an errand. When he returned, he was carrying a guitar case.

"Consuelo and I want to give you this as a farewell gift, Juan." He handed him the case.

As Juan opened the case and took out a guitar, Margie's father added, "When you told us that your guitar had been stolen in Chicago, you tried to make light of it. But I can imagine it must have hurt. A good player like you should never be without a guitar."

Juan thanked his brother-in-law with a hug.

"Why don't you play for the girls?" Margie's mother said. "They can show you the dances they have been practicing in the *folklórico* class at school."

"Well, which dances are those?" Juan replied. For a long while, he played all the songs that the girls named, as they stomped and whirled, following the lively steps of the *folklórico* dances.

# 19. Dress Rehearsal

At school it was getting harder to stay focused as the days grew warmer. Even Camille, who usually paid attention to every word the teacher said, seemed distracted. Instead of telling Margie all the new facts she had discovered on the Internet about dolphins, whales, or manatees, she doodled flowers and butterflies all over her notebook.

Most of the school day Margie felt as if she was about to fall asleep. If she looked out the window, she imagined herself floating on top of a cloud. But when classes ended, she woke up again for the *folklórico* practice.

Mrs. Rodríguez now had them practicing every day for the Cinco de Mayo celebration. It was going to be a big performance to showcase the dances they had been learning all year.

True to her word, Mrs. Rodríguez had made Margie an understudy. Margie had looked the word up in the dictionary and discovered that in spite of the prefix "under," this was something to take pride in. An understudy, she learned, is an actor or a dancer who is trained to take over the part of a leading actor or dancer if the need arises. Whenever any of the girls was absent, Margie would take her place. But even when all the girls were present, from time to time Mrs. Rodríguez would let one of them rest awhile so that Margie could fill in. This way Margie would always be ready to take over during a performance, should she be needed.

"Aren't you coming back to help in the library anymore?" Camille asked one afternoon.

"Please tell Ms. Faggioni that I'll be back next week. The practices for Cinco de Mayo will be over by then," Margie answered as she rushed to the other end of the school.

That afternoon, practice seemed to last longer than ever. Afterward Mrs. Rodríguez gave them all juice and apple slices as a snack. Then she made an announcement.

"On Thursday we will be practicing in the auditorium. Will all of you please bring your costumes? We will be having a full dress rehearsal on Friday. It would be great if some of your mothers could come that day to help you get dressed and braid your hair."

"Well . . . good-bye, Mrs. Rodríguez," said Margie. "I guess I won't be coming back. I don't have a costume. Lupe's mother is sending hers from Mexico, but I'm not truly Mexican, you know. I was born—"

"Yes, I know, you were born in Texas. But please, do come anyway. I'm sure not everyone will have their costumes yet. And you know the steps so well that it would be wonderful if you could assist us, Margarita."

Then she added softly, "It's such a joy to see you dance." Those words echoed sweetly in Margie's mind as she skipped, ran, and twirled all the way home.

# 20. Ribbons from Mexico

When the package arrived the next day, Lupe was taking a shower, so it was Margie who opened the door for the delivery person, a young woman with dozens of brightly beaded braids in her hair.

"What a huge package," she said to Margie with a smile. "I hope it's going to make someone very happy."

"It's for my cousin. It's her dress for a Cinco de Mayo dance recital."

"Oh, wow! I've always loved Cinco de Mayo," the young woman replied. "The traditional Mexican dances are so lively, and those dresses with the wide skirts are so beautiful. I've always wondered, do the colors of the dresses have any meaning?"

"I don't really know," Margie answered, "but I don't think so. I think it's pretty much whatever the dancers want to wear, or maybe it's whatever their mothers want them to wear! I heard some of the girls mention that their mothers wanted their daughters' dresses to be the same colors as theirs were when they were young."

"And you, what color is your dress?"

"I . . . I don't have one. I'm not dancing. I've only been filling in for some of the girls when they are absent." She stopped for a moment, then continued, "I'm not really Mexican anyway. I'm American. I was born in Texas. . . ."

"I never knew you needed to be Mexican to dance *folklórico*," the young woman answered. "I've always dreamt of learning it myself. I still might, someday." She spun around with a dreamy look in her eyes, sending her beads into a joyful jingle. "Well, I have to go now. It was nice talking to you. *¡Feliz Cinco de Mayo!*" Laughing, she added, "It's an American holiday, you know!"

After the delivery woman left, Margie rushed upstairs and knocked on the bathroom door. "Just in case you want to know, the package with your costume is here!"

Her words had the intended effect. A few seconds later Lupe was flying down the stairs with her long black hair wrapped in a towel.

"Hurry! Let's open it!" said Margie.

"Do you think it's all right to open it without waiting for your mother to come home?" There was concern in Lupe's voice.

"It's addressed to you," Margie said, but then she hesitated. "Still, I'm sure Mami would appreciate it if we waited."

Consuelo had been enjoying her classes at the community college very much. Now she was talking about the possibility of enrolling in a dental hygienist program after completing two more semesters of English.

"I never thought that I could have a profession," she had commented one morning at breakfast. "But you girls are being such a big help around the house, and all of us could certainly benefit if I started bringing home a good paycheck."

Lupe had looked at her uncle to see his reaction. She had heard some of her classmates mention that their fathers would not want their mothers to work outside the home. But her uncle did not seem upset. Instead he was looking at his wife with pride.

Now Lupe said, "Tía Consuelo is always doing nice things for us. I don't think I could have survived so far away from home if your mother weren't so kind! Let's wait for her before we open the package."

While Margie was glad they were choosing to wait, it seemed as though her mother was taking forever.

At last Margie heard her mother opening the door. "It's here, Mami! Lupe's package is here!" she called out with excitement.

"Did you open it?"

"No, Mami, we waited for you."

"That was very nice. Let's see. . . ."

The girls handed her a pair of scissors, and Consuelo deftly opened the package. From beneath a huge cloud of white tissue paper Consuelo pulled out a gorgeous purple dress. The ribbons along the top of the blouse and around the wide skirt were many different shades of pink and violet.

"How beautiful, Lupe! You'll be the prettiest dancer ever. And with your long braids, you'll be just perfect!" Margie's enthusiasm took both her mother and her cousin by surprise.

Lupe looked at the dress, and her eyes grew misty with tears. "It must have taken my mother such a long time to sew this dress," she said. "When Abuelita Mercedes moved to my uncle's house, she gave my mother her sewing machine. The first thing my mother sewed on it was that dress I wore the first day of school. Do you remember my pink dress, Margie?"

"Of course I remember," answered Margie. "It was only eight months ago, although it feels like it's been ages!"

"Well, let's see what else is here," said Margie's mother as she took out another layer of paper. Then she lifted out another dress. This one was white, with red and blue ribbons. Pinned to it was a note in Spanish.

Lupe read the note aloud, translating it into English:

*Dear American niece Margarita:*

*I hope you enjoy dancing in this dress. I made it white like the flower that you are named after, and I also added the colors of the country where you were born. May this dress make you happy. Thank you for being kind to my Lupita. Maybe after she finishes learning English, you can come back with her and spend some time with us.*

*Your Mexican aunt,*
*Dolores*

"Oh, Lupe, your mother is so nice," said Margie as she hugged her cousin. "Mami, you knew all along, didn't you? Even if I don't have a part in the dance, I will still wear this dress on Cinco de Mayo. It's much too pretty to stay in a box. Of course, it's going to look funny with my short hair."

"No, no, it won't. Most of the girls don't have hair that long either, and many of them will be wearing braids made of black yarn," said Lupe. "You'll be just fine. *¿Verdad, Tía?* Isn't that so?"

"Of course," answered Tía Consuelo. "Just wait and see what we can do with these!" she added as she pulled out several handfuls of colored ribbons from the very bottom of the package.

# 21. Margie? Margarita?

When Margie and her family walked into the school auditorium for the Cinco de Mayo celebration, Margie marveled at how many people had come. Somehow she had not expected that so many of her teachers and classmates would turn out to watch the performance.

"Wow! You look gorgeous!" said Betty as Margie walked up the side aisle toward the stage.

"Can we take a picture with you after the show?" asked Liz.

Margie smiled, realizing that most of her classmates were sitting together.

"Of course, I'll wait for you. I'm not dancing tonight."

"That's because you're not really Mexican, right Margareeeta?" John chimed in.

"Better leave her alone, John. You're not that funny, you know," said Camille. "If you want to make people laugh, why don't you learn some new jokes? Go find some joke books in the library or something."

"See you later, guys. I'm going backstage in case Mrs. Rodríguez needs some help." Margie practically floated up the aisle.

Mrs. Rodríguez greeted her with a smile. "You look beautiful, Margarita! What an amazing dress!"

"My aunt, Lupe's mother, sent it from Mexico."

"It's magnificent. You'll look great on stage."

"But I'm not dancing! Mrs. Rodríguez, is someone sick? Who's absent?"

"Nobody is sick, don't worry. Just take your place at the center of the line."

"But . . . that's Lupe's place."

"Well, not tonight. Tonight it's yours. Hurry now. We're about to begin."


Mrs. Rodríguez greeted the audience: "*Buenas noches.* Good evening. *Bienvenidos a nuestra celebración del Cinco de Mayo.* We hope you will enjoy the program we have prepared for you. Our students have worked very hard all year to bring you the joy and beauty of these Mexican traditions. But before we begin to dance, one of our students has a very special presentation.

"Music comes in many different forms, and sometimes the words of a poem can create a music all their own. One of our students, Lupe González, will show us how the great poet Rubén Darío used language to create music. On the back of your program you will find an English translation of the poem that Lupe will be reciting for us tonight in Spanish. Whether you speak Spanish or not, we invite you to listen and enjoy the sounds of this poem."

As the curtains opened, Lupe stood silently center stage, looking radiant in her beautiful purple dress. After bowing to the audience, she began by saying, *"A Margarita."*

Margie was so surprised at first that she could barely follow Lupe's voice. As Mrs. Rodríguez had said, it sounded very melodious, but she hardly understood any of the words. Yet as Lupe began telling the story of the king who had a diamond palace, a tent made of sunlight, a malachite kiosk, and an entire herd of elephants, the words started to sound more familiar.

A profound silence settled over the auditorium as the story of the little princess unfolded. Margie, Margarita, was afraid that it was so quiet that everyone could hear her heart thumping as she stood backstage with the other dancers. Meanwhile, Lupe continued to tell how the princess traveled up to the sky, beyond the moon, searching for the shining star she so wanted.

To Margie it seemed as though she were hearing the musical sounds of the Spanish language for the first time. Lupe's voice reminded her of her own mother's, lulling her to sleep when she was very young, and the words felt as warm and soft as her mother's caresses.

Suddenly Lupe raised her voice to show how angry the king was when the princess returned home with the star. He had been worried about her, as he did not know where she had gone, and now he was very angry that she had dared to bring a star home from the heavens. Margie felt the urgency in Lupe's voice fill the room with suspense.

Then Lupe's voice changed again, to the sweet tones of the little princess, who was trying to explain that she had meant no harm. Margie marveled at Lupe's ability to change voices. She'd never realized that her cousin had this kind of talent.

Now Margie heard the voice of the king once more as he demanded in thundering tones that the princess return the star. Margie realized she felt bad for the princess. After having found a star—*una flor de luz*, a "flower made of light," the poet had called it—would the princess really have to return it? How sad! Lupe's voice captured everyone's attention as the story reached its end.

Margie, Margarita, sighed with pleasure. She liked happy endings and was relieved that the princess would get to keep her star. She enjoyed seeing Lupe standing tall and self-assured, speaking loudly and clearly, holding everyone spellbound with the beauty of the poem. Then Margarita heard her name once more. And how different her own name, Margarita, sounded!

As the poem ended with the poet saying good-bye to the girl to whom he had dedicated the poem, it seemed to Margie as though the words were being addressed directly to her, as though she herself were the Margarita in the poem.

Then Lupe was bowing, applause filled the auditorium, and Margarita felt herself straightening up as she realized that at any moment it would be the dancers' turn to go on stage.

The curtains reopened, displaying what looked like an enormous bouquet of spectacular flowers, with the dancers standing in their starting positions, holding their ample ribboned skirts up to form a blossoming rainbow of colors.

Music filled the air as the girls in the front line began marking the rhythm on the floor with their dance shoes, accompanied by the boys, who formed a second line behind them. Soon there were couples moving back and forth all over the stage. As the smooth fabric of her white dress swirled, Margarita felt the love of her family enveloping her, especially the love of her mother, who had given her the name of a flower—the name that also belonged to a girl from long ago, the girl to whom a poet had dedicated his beautiful poem. And as Margarita whirled and twirled, she saw her blue and red ribbons swirling, the colors that her aunt had chosen in honor of the land where Margarita was born.

The more she danced, the more she knew in her heart that she was both Margie and Margarita, American and Mexican. She could be proud of everything good about Mexico—the loving people, the lively music, the spirited dances, the vivid paintings her cousin had shown her. And she also could be proud of everything good about the United States— the beautiful places she still dreamed of visiting, the library where she could find any book she wanted, her school, her teachers, the kind librarian, and her wonderful friends. She did not need to give up anything to celebrate the best of her two countries: the country where she was born and the country where her family's roots had grown.

Soon she'd visit Mexico with Lupe and learn everything she could about the land of her parents. She might even travel all over the world, knowing that good people are everywhere and that who you are is not where you were born, but what is in your heart. Knowing now that she'd found the words to express what was truly important to her, she felt the music sweeping her along, a white *margarita* decked with red and blue, blossoming more fully with each step of her Mexican dance.

# "My Family"
### by Margarita "Margie" Ceballos-González

*I have always been proud of being born in
the United States of America. I was born
in Texas, and I lived there until I was in
second grade, when we moved to California.
At first I thought I would write about being
American, because it seemed like that was
the most important thing to me.*

*I am American, but my family is
Mexican. For a long time this was confusing
to me. I love my family. My parents have
always loved me and taken care of me. I
know that I am very lucky to have them.*

*But my parents are not from the United
States. They speak Spanish, and they do
things differently than most of my friends'
parents because their culture is different
too. Even though they have learned English,*

they speak with an accent. I think they will always be more Mexican than American.

For a long time I tried hard to get them to be more American. I was afraid of being different. I wanted to fit in. I thought that because I was born here and I speak English well, I was not like the students in the bilingual class, who have just arrived in this country and do not speak any English yet. I did not want to speak Spanish, even at home, and that made my parents sad.

Then my cousin came to live with us. She was born in Mexico, and she did not speak any English when she first came here. It was hard because some of the kids at school started teasing me again.

At home my parents started talking in Spanish a lot with my cousin. Sometimes I felt like she was closer to them than I was. Sometimes I felt left out, even though they weren't trying to make me feel that way.

I know that things have been hard for my cousin, too. It has been hard for her to learn a new language and a new way of life. But she is learning to be in both worlds, and she seems to really like it. Now she is like a sister to me, and I have never had a sister before.

My cousin's parents are separated, and that is why she came to live with us in the first place. Her mother and her grandmother and her twin brothers are in Mexico, and she loves them very much. I think she will also visit her father's new family in Texas someday. Yet she has decided to stay here with me and my parents, and I am really happy about that.

What I have learned is that sometimes good things can come from change, even if it is hard at first. When my family changed, it was not easy, but now I have a cousin who is my sister. My cousin is Mexican, and she is learning English and learning how to enjoy living in the United States. I am American, and I am learning more Spanish and learning more about Mexico, too.

Like my dolphin-loving friend Camille says, almost everyone's family came here from somewhere else, even if they like to pretend that they have always been here. I don't want to pretend anymore.

*My name is Margarita, which means "daisy" in Spanish. My mother gave me my name because she loves flowers, and she knew that I would love flowers too. I love my Mexican family, my Mexican name, and* folklórico *dancing.*

*I am American because I was born here, and now I know that I am also Mexican because my parents are Mexican. I love my family and my friends very much. I have relatives who live in Mexico, and I also have relatives who live in the United States.*

*This is what I want people to understand: I am American, and I am Mexican. Both are important to me and neither one has to be better than the other. I am very lucky to be both. I am also very lucky to have my family, especially my mom, my dad, and my new sister, Lupe.*

# A Margarita

por Rubén Darío

# To Margarita

by Rubén Darío

English translation by
Rosalma Zubizarreta

Margarita, está linda la mar,
    y el viento
    lleva esencia sutil de azahar;
    yo siento
en el alma una alondra cantar:
    tu acento.
Margarita, te voy a contar
    un cuento.

Este era un rey que tenía
    un palacio de diamantes,
    una tienda hecha del día
    y un rebaño de elefantes,
    un quiosco de malaquita,
    un gran manto de tisú,
    y una gentil princesita,
    tan bonita,
    Margarita,
    tan bonita como tú.
Una tarde la princesa
    vio una estrella aparecer;
    la princesa era traviesa
    y la quiso ir a coger.

Margarita, the sea is so lovely today,
    and the gentle breeze
    brings the soft scent of neroli.
    Somewhere in my soul
    There's a lark that sings in full glory.
    I hear the sound of your name . . .
    Margarita,
    I'd like to tell you a story.

Once there was a mighty king
    with a palace made of diamonds,
    a tent made out of daylight,
    and an entire herd of elephants,
    a malachite kiosk,
    a cloak made of the finest silks,
    and a gentle princess for a daughter,
    a lovely daughter,
    Margarita,
    who was as beautiful as you.
One evening the little princess
    saw a star up in the sky;
    being very brave and daring,
    she thought she would—at least she'd try—

La quería para hacerla
    decorar un prendedor,
    con un verso y una perla,
    y una pluma y una flor.
Las princesas primorosas
    se parecen mucho a ti:
    cortan lirios, cortan rosas,
    cortan astros. Son así.
Pues se fue la niña bella
    bajo el cielo y sobre el mar,
    a cortar la blanca estrella
    que la hacía suspirar.
Y siguió camino arriba,
    por la luna y más allá;
    mas lo malo es que ella iba
    sin permiso del papá.
Cuando estuvo ya de vuelta
    de los parques del Señor,
    se miraba toda envuelta
    en un dulce resplandor.
Y el rey dijo: —¿Qué te has hecho?
    Te he buscado y no te hallé.
    Y, ¿qué tienes en el pecho,
    que encendido se te ve?

To find the star and bring it home
for a brooch that she was making,
with a poem and a pearl,
and a feather and a flower.
Ah, those dainty princesses
who are very much like you:
They cut lilies, they cut roses,
they cut stars. That's what they do. . . .
Well, the lovely girl went out
beneath the sky and over the sea,
in search of the shining star
upon which she'd set her heart.
Higher and higher she climbed,
past the moon and far beyond;
yet the trouble was she had forgotten
to ask her father if she might go.
When at last she had returned
from the fields of the good Lord,
she was beaming, she was radiant,
she was wrapped in a sweet glow.
Then her father asked: "Where were you?
I searched for you, both high and low.
And what is that you're wearing,
what lovely gem that sparkles so?"

La princesa no mentía,
   y así, dijo la verdad:
   —Fui a cortar la estrella mía
   a la azul inmensidad.
Y el rey clama: —¿No te he dicho
   que el azul no hay que tocar?
   ¡Qué locura! ¡Qué capricho!
   El Señor se va a enojar.
Y ella dice: —No hubo intento;
   yo me fui no sé por qué;
   por las olas y en el viento
   fui a la estrella y la corté.
Y el papá dice enojado:
   —Un castigo has de tener:
   vuelve al cielo, y lo robado
   vas ahora a devolver.
La princesa se entristece
   por su dulce flor de luz,
   cuando entonces aparece
   sonriendo el buen Jesús.
Y así dice: —En mis campiñas
   esa rosa le ofrecí:
   son mis flores de las niñas
   que al soñar piensan en mí.

The princess could not tell a lie,
      and so instead she told the truth:
      "I went out to the blue yonder
      to find the right star for my brooch."
The king is angry with his daughter:
      "Oh, what foolishness is this!
      Haven't I warned you often enough?
      You risk the wrath of our good Lord
      by daring to harvest the skies above."
Then the princess answers softly:
      "I didn't mean to cause any harm.
      I rode the waves, I rode the wind,
      I found the star and brought it home."
To which her father answers sternly:
      "It's time to pay for what you've done.
      You must go back with what you've stolen.
      Back to the sky it must return."
The princess now is gazing sadly
      at her lovely flower of light,
      when suddenly appears before them
      the good Lord Jesus, in all his might.
Smiling gently at them both,
      he soon sets their hearts at ease:
      "I have given her this rose
      as I wandered through my fields:

*Viste el rey ropas brillantes,*
   *y luego hace desfilar*
   *cuatrocientos elefantes*
   *a la orilla de la mar.*
*La princesita está bella,*
   *pues ya tiene el prendedor*
   *en que lucen, con la estrella,*
   *verso, perla, pluma y flor.*

*Margarita, está linda la mar,*
   *y el viento*
   *lleva esencia sutil de azahar:*
   *tu aliento.*
*Ya que lejos de mí vas a estar,*
   *guarda, niña, un gentil pensamiento*
   *a quien un día te quiso contar*
   *un cuento.*

All my flowers belong to those
who keep me in their thoughts and dreams."
The king is garbed in all his finest
and has ordered by decree
all four hundred of his elephants
parading by the edge of the sea.
The lovely princess looks quite radiant
as she wears her finest brooch,
upon which shine, next to her star,
a feather and a flower, a poem and a pearl.

Margarita, the sea is so lovely today
and the gentle breeze
brings the soft scent of neroli.
I hear the sound of your sigh.
Since you shall be far and away, dear girl,
please keep in your heart a kind thought
for him who one day sought
to please you by telling a story.

# About "To Margarita"/ "A Margarita"
## by Rubén Darío

In 1908, Rubén Darío was invited by Luis A. Debayle, a well-known medical doctor in Nicaragua, to visit his family at their summer home on Isla del Cardón. During his stay, Margarita Debayle, Luis's five-year-old daughter, asked the poet for a story. In response, Darío penned the verses that would later become one of the best-known poems in the Spanish language.

A tribute to beauty in its many forms, the story celebrates the innocence of the little princess whose heartfelt desire allows her to pick a star as though it were a flower. The poem also honors the poet's own creative drive, as he recognizes that "somewhere in my soul, there's a lark that sings in full glory" and hopes that, in return for his efforts, he will be remembered with kindness.

Translating Darío is a daunting task, in part due to his masterful and complex use of rhyme and rhythm. Rather than a strict translation, Rosalma Zubizarreta has sought to create a new and accessible English version. While respecting the original content as much as possible, she has also adapted the text as needed to convey some of the playfulness and musicality of the original poem.